Elio

A Possessive Second Chance Dark Mafia Billionaire Romance

Calabresi Mafia
Book 4

L.K. Ryan

 Created with Vellum

Acknowledgments

This book wouldn't happen without the support of my amazing readers. I can't thank you enough.

Calabresi Family

Family Map:

Elio Calabresi - Father, Retired Don
Adelina Calabresi - Mother
Savio Calabresi - Boss
Sante Calabresi - Underboss
Renato Calabresi - Enforcer
Elio III - Consigliere
Vincenzo - CEO of Calabresi Holdings

Disclaimer

Warning: There are a few scenes that may trigger. Be aware. Contains strong language and explicit sexual content and is only intended for mature readers. A Dark Mafia Billionaire romance with an asshole alpha male, possessive and aggressive. This story may contain unconventional situations, language, and sexual encounters that may offend some readers. This book is for mature readers (18+).

Introduction

Are you signed up for my newsletter?

Join today and find out all the latest in new releases, contests, giveaways, sneak peeks, and more.

www.authorlkryan.com

Synopsis

Elio

I wasn't supposed to take it this far; I was young and thought I knew what love was, but she couldn't be mine forever. She hates me for what I did and reminds me every time I see her that I'll never have her again.

Cora

I've known him since my mother worked for his family and loved him since we were young. The Calabresi rules were in place from the beginning, and our worlds could never collide again after he broke my heart.

Will Elio convince Cora that his love for her never faded? Or will it be too late when her life hangs in the balance?

A second chance, possessive hero, hate to love, forbidden, Dark Mafia romance. Book 4 in an interconnecting stand-alone series with a guaranteed HEA.

Chapter 1

Elio Jr

Six months later

Christmas Eve 2022

It was our annual holiday dinner with family and friends at my parents' house. When my older brothers started having kids, they wanted to create their own family traditions on Christmas Day, so Mom insisted on hosting a dinner every Christmas Eve.

Cora and I had done this dinner together for years before we'd broken up. We'd slept here, woken up together, had breakfast, and exchanged gifts.

But things were very different now.

I slipped into the bathroom and locked the door behind me. My eyes skimmed Cora's body, and my chest throbbed painfully at the thought of her dating someone else.

I stalked over to her at the sink as she washed her hands.

"Get out!" Cora pressed her hand against my chest and tried to push me away.

I grabbed her hand and kissed the back of her palm. "You didn't answer my call."

"EJ, leave me alone."

As she brushed past me, I wrapped my arm around her waist, pulling her to my chest. "I'm sorry," I whispered, kissing her shoulder.

"You're ten years too late." Cora unlocked the door and slipped out of my reach.

"Fuck!" I smacked everything off the counter, and it crashed to the floor.

Beyond pissed, I stomped out of the bathroom. I glanced around the hallway of my parent's home and spotted Cora talking with my mother and my sister-in-law, Rena.

A hand on my chest stopped me from moving in their direction. "Leave her alone," Savio warned.

My gaze clashed with Cora's as Savio extended his arm around my shoulder, and she rolled her eyes. For the past few days, I'd called, sent texts, and even showed up at her house, all to no avail. The avoidance had to stop. I was ready to take action.

I shrugged Savio off. "She's been avoiding me. I'm done playing games."

"Cora's like a sister to our family. Give her some time," he advised.

"She saw me at a club with a few women."

"And let me guess. You saw her with a guy and ran him off."

I inhaled a steadying breath. "She's too young to date."

"She's twenty-four, EJ," Savio said.

I ran a hand down my face in frustration. I didn't regret pushing men away when they got too close to Cora. "We're friends."

I followed Savio into my father's office and plopped down on the couch, rubbing my throbbing temples as he shut the door.

Savio sat in the chair. "Friends, my ass. Stop being an idiot. I have other things to discuss."

"Where's Pops?"

"Playing with the kids in the backyard." He gestured to the window before returning his gaze to me. "I need you to go to New York. Giosuè needs some assistance."

I scrutinized him. "How long?"

"Not sure. Probably a few weeks. The situation with Gallagher needs to be dealt with."

"I'll get Vaughn and Thompson to clear us if there's any blowback."

"Something is happening, EJ, and the question is, are you ready for it? I'm not sure what's going on with you and Cora, but you need a clear head."

"Leave it alone." Now was not the time to talk about my personal life.

"Don't hurt her. Cora and Marilyn mean a lot to our family," Savio warned, referring to Cora's mom.

"I'll kill myself before I hurt her." I glared as I followed him out of the office.

"Cora, why are you so dressed up?" Rena asked.

"I have a date," Cora answered.

I marched over to her at the dining room table. "No, you fucking don't!"

"Why do you care, EJ?" Rena demanded.

I flipped her off.

Cora's nostrils flared. "None of your business."

"Whoever he is, say goodbye because we're gonna send him to an early grave and pay for his funeral."

Cora jumped up from her seat as the doorbell rang.

"Are you ready?" an unfamiliar voice asked as she opened the door.

"What the fuck?" I marched behind her and yanked the door wide. Removing my gun from the holster, I pointed it at his head.

Cora's date threw his hands in the air, and his eyes skittered between Cora and me.

"Elio Jr!" my mother yelled.

Cora jumped in front of the gun. "Put that away," she spat, trying to force my hand down.

"Move, Cora," I growled.

"No. You've lost your mind." Cora pushed against my chest.

I moved back and put my gun away.

"You know better, son," my father stated, his mouth tight with disapproval.

I'd given Cora space and kept things friendly during family gatherings. I knew I didn't deserve her, but I was done with the games. "He needs to leave."

"Your nephews are watching. Stop this right now," Mother hissed.

Her words finally penetrated, and I realized I'd gone too far. I relaxed but stared at the smug look on her date's face.

I reached for Cora's hand as she left the house. "If you leave this house, we'll have a big problem."

Cora froze. "My life is no longer your concern."

I moved toward the bastard. I wanted to wring his neck.

"Let her go." Renato clamped a hand on my shoulder.

"Get off me." I shoved him back.

"Marilyn is family, and you're acting like an ass." Mother shook her head in disappointment.

Everybody watched Cora leave with him like they were a happy couple.

They pissed me off even more. I wanted to reach for my gun again but had another idea. Grabbing my jacket off the coat rack, I jogged outside to my Ferrari as Cora and her date pulled out of the driveway.

Before I could start the engine, the door opened, and Renato climbed in next to me.

"What the fuck are you doing?"

"Here to make sure you don't do anything stupid," Renato replied coolly.

I pressed the gas pedal and drove to the main road, watching the car in the front head in the opposite direction to Cora's place. I reached into my pocket and pulled out my phone, texting one of the guards we always had on Cora.

Me: *Make sure he ends the date asap.*

Freddie: *If he refuses?*

Me: *Kill him.*

Freddie: *Accident or...?*

Me: *Doesn't matter.*

I smiled and re-pocketed my phone. Turning up the music, I lit a cigarette.

Renato went to turn the radio down.

I smacked his hand away. "I don't want to talk." I knew what I was about to do was wrong, but I didn't care.

"Whatever you just did will only piss her off even more," Renato pointed out.

"Better she's pissed off and safe at home than with him," I muttered.

"It's about time you got over her and moved on."

I glared at him. Renato, of all people, had no right to tell me to get over a woman.

"Where are we going, by the way?" Renato questioned.

"I need to grab some files from my office."

"It's Christmas Eve. No one works on Christmas Eve," Renato said.

"Well, no one asked you to jump in my car. You should've stayed back at the house."

As the third eldest, Renato wanted to play the saint. "Someone had to ensure you didn't kill him or yourself." He snatched away my cigarette.

"Why do you fucking care, Dr. Phil? Sitting there, all calm and collected. You think because you've got a wife and kid, you can give relationship advice?"

"Nothing about me is calm and collected. I just know how to put the craziness aside, dear brother. Unlike you, it seems.

Arriving at the Calabresi building, I parked out front instead of in my usual reserved spot.

Renato threw a hand in the air. "Are you really gonna work on Christmas Eve?"

"Yeah. If I gotta fly to New York and handle this bullshit with Cade Gallagher."

"Gallagher will get touched."

I nodded in agreement as we climbed out of the car. Andrew, one of the security guards on duty, raised a hand to acknowledge us.

Renato pushed the glass door open, and I followed him to the elevator. He hated the nine-to-five lifestyle. As

Enforcer, he got the call when we needed a person handled.

I took care of the legalities. I was the second youngest son and trained in all aspects of the Calabresi mafia world. As the Consigliere, it was my duty to ensure none of our names came up in any dealings. When they needed an extra pair of hands to get rid of someone, I was more than equipped to handle myself. Everyone underestimated me because I wore suits and could talk with presidents of countries and Fortune Five Hundred CEOs as easily as local drug dealers on the streets who sold nickel and dime bags.

But when it concerned Cora, I turned into EJ Calabresi, son of a mobster.

We stepped off the elevator and strolled down the hall to my floor, which housed the legal department.

I slipped the key into the door, and the light automatically came on as I stepped inside my office. "What the...?"

The place was trashed.

Renato entered behind me and looked around in shock. He pulled out his gun. "What the fuck, EJ?"

I reached for the desk phone to call security. "Get up here now," I barked into the receiver.

"Shit. Looks like you've made an enemy," Renato said. "You pissed off someone?"

A flicker of annoyance popped into my head, and I knew this wasn't a random act. I'd fired my last assistant, Angelina, for fucking up constantly and coming in late all the time. She'd been recommended by Vincenzo, but I think he'd slept with her a few times and fobbed her off on me when she'd screwed up in accounting.

"Shit." I cursed.

Renato narrowed his eyes. "You keep anything important here?"

I knew he was asking if I had any mafia paperwork at the office. "No. I'm careful." Calabresi Holdings only kept essential paperwork. I kept my mafia dealings in a safe at home.

"You called, Boss?" Andrew, the security guy, asked as he appeared in the doorway.

I checked my computer. Nothing seemed off. I picked up the pens and staples on the desk. "Did anyone leave here in a rush?"

Andrew responded, "No, sir."

"Have you made the rounds tonight?" Renato asked.

Andrew's hands clenched into fists at his sides. "I was still checking the first floor. I can call the police."

"Did you see anything suspicious? Maybe Angelina?" I asked, recalling that she worked late.

Andrew frowned. "Angelina from accounting?"

"Yeah, did she come by recently?"

"Not unless she came before my shift. I've been here since the office closed two days ago."

Renato's phone rang, and he moved away to answer it.

"I need the security footage sent to me," I told Andrew.

He nodded. "Yes, Boss. But... are you sure we shouldn't call the police?"

"No police. Just get the footage."

"Fuck!" Renato exploded as he talked on the phone. "Yeah, I'm with him now."

"What's up?" I asked, stepping around the desk and walking toward him.

Renato's expression was grim as he ended the call.

"What happened?"

Renato took in a shuddering breath. It was difficult for him to make eye contact with me. "That was Savio."

"And?" The only thing that would have Renato so off-kilter was if something had happened to a family member. Mafia business wouldn't have him this upset.

"Cora was in a car accident."

I closed my eyes and counted to three to calm my nerves, but it didn't help. "Where is she?"

"They're taking her to Amory Memorial."

I pulled my phone out of my pocket. "Her date?" I asked through gritted teeth as we hurried to the elevator. We stepped in as soon as the doors opened, my trashed office forgotten.

"Apparently, he was speeding. Savio said Marilyn was on her way to the hospital. Mom has a driver taking her," Renato explained, referring to Cora's mom.

"I want him dead."

"We don't know if he was the cause," he reasoned.

My patience was wearing thin as I repeatedly stabbed the lobby button. "You just said he was speeding."

This goddamn elevator was taking too long.

Renato gripped my shoulder and nudged me out of the way. "Calm the fuck down. Cora will be fine. Acting recklessly will only put you in the hospital, too."

I shoved him off me as the doors finally opened. As soon as we reached the lobby, I jogged out of the building to the car.

Renato grabbed me as I reached the driver's side. "Give me the keys. I'll drive."

"I'm fine."

He extended a hand. "You're pissed and upset."

"I said I'm fine," I gritted through my teeth.

"You're not fine. We can stand here wasting time, or

you can let me drive so we get to the hospital in one piece."

I glared at him but finally relented. "All right, you drive." I tossed the keys to him.

"Calm down and relax. She needs you with your head on straight," Renato said as I climbed into the passenger seat beside him and pulled out my phone.

"You're right." Acting out and being pissed about a date wouldn't help the situation. I had to show her I'd changed.

I took some deep breaths to regulate my breathing. Cold sweat trickled down my spine. Cora held my heart in her hands. If someone had hurt her, I'd move heaven and earth to make them pay.

A few minutes later, we arrived at the hospital. I ran inside and went straight to the reception desk. "I'm here looking for Cora—"

"EJ! Over here!" Savio's voice cut me off, and I turned to see him in the waiting area with Sante.

"Is she alive?" I asked immediately.

Savio planted a hand on my shoulder with a somber look. "They haven't come out to tell us anything yet. Mom is back there with Marilyn, talking to the doctors."

I was glad Mom was with Cora's mother. "What do we know?"

"Just that the car was speeding and ran a red light," Sante replied. His gaze swept over Renato and me. "Cora's date was driving. I guess they were arguing over you."

"Where is he now?" I turned to find him, but Sante and Renato pushed me back to the waiting area.

"He's being treated," Sante explained.

My lungs seized at the thought of Cora being harmed. "I want him taken."

Sante grunted, "We can't just take him from the hospital."

"We're Calabresis. We can do whatever the fuck we want. He's a fuck boy."

Savio saw the fire in my eyes. "We'll see what we can do."

Before I could say anything more, Marylin and my mom appeared.

I rushed over and hugged both women. "How is she?"

"Sore, but she's going to be fine," Mom explained.

"She's resting now. I'm going to grab her something to eat," Marilyn answered.

"Where are the kids?" I asked.

"Your father's watching them," Mom responded.

"Can she have visitors?" I wanted to see that she was okay with my own eyes.

Chapter 2

Elio Jr

Savio told Sante to go with Mom and ensure Marilyn had everything she needed for Cora. Renato was left making calls to take care of our little problem in the other room. If her date didn't die from the car accident, I'd make it a reality some other way.

Hearing Cora breathing through the machine caused me to hesitate as I approached her bed. The moment we were in a room together, I was driven to touch her in some way. All those moments of pretending we were just friends ended today. She couldn't run from me anymore. I was no longer content to settle for friendship. Never had been.

Seeing her lying helpless and injured was my worst nightmare. This should never have happened. I wanted answers from Freddie, her security. He'd better be ready to give me all the details, or his life would be in jeopardy. Cora hated having bodyguards, but all the women in our family were assigned protection around the clock. Most of the time, Cora made them stay outside in the car, despite our demands to be in her business twenty-four-seven.

Cora had always been independent, even at fourteen when we met. She was cute, with her brunette pigtails, braces, and wide eyes, but it was her smart mouth that captivated me. When Marilyn came to work for us during the summer, Cora tagged along and hung out with us, trying to do everything my brothers and I did.

"What are you doing here?" Cora stirred and sat up slowly.

I drew closer to help, but she held a hand out to stop me. I grasped her hand and stroked my thumb over her palm. "I came as soon as I heard."

"You can go." She refused to look at me.

"Cora—"

"My mother is here, so you can leave," she cut me off, shifting her weight with a grimace.

"I wanted to see you," I said, blowing out a heavy breath.

Her cheeks flushed in her pale face. "You shouldn't be here."

"What did the doctor say?" I asked, ignoring her comment.

The door opened before she could reply. I turned to see the doctor enter the room with a nurse behind him.

"I see you're awake," the doctor said with a smile. He approached her bed and picked up the chart.

"When can I go home?"

"What happened to her?"

Cora and I spoke at the same time.

The doctor looked from me to Cora. "I'm sorry. I didn't know your husband was here."

"He's not—"

"I got the call and came immediately," I interrupted before she could answer.

Cora's eyes widened, and she snatched her hand from mine. The doctor cleared his throat as Cora folded her arms and ignored me. Her stubbornness only made me want to break through the walls she'd erected around her.

"He's not my husband," she told the doctor emphatically. "Please tell me when I can leave."

I cleared my throat. "Can I talk to you in private for a moment?" I clapped him on the back and walked him out of the room. "Cora's a little stubborn, but I'd appreciate you keeping me in the loop on everything that concerns her," I told him once we were outside the corridor.

He frowned. "As you're not a relative, I can't do that for legal reasons."

I checked the corridor for witnesses before my smile dropped and was replaced with a scowl. "I could ruin your career with one phone call, but I'd rather not do that, doctor."

He swallowed hard and nodded. "She's going to be fine. Just a little bump on her head."

"Bump on her head from what?"

He flipped through the chart. "A mugger, or so she says."

A mugger? What the fuck?

I schooled my features to hide my shock and summoned a smile. "Thanks."

I returned to the hospital room as the nurse left.

Cora lifted accusing eyes to mine. "Did you threaten him?"

"If I answer that, you'll be pissed."

"You promised to stay out of my life." Cora wrapped her arms around herself.

I reached out to rub her leg. "I never promised that."

"Please go, EJ. I'll be fine."

"I'm taking you home."

"No," she spat, shaking her head.

"Why do you continue to fight me?"

"I'm sleepy. I'd like you to leave, please." Cora squeezed her hands into fists.

I sighed and nodded. I didn't want to push her anymore when she was injured. I bent to kiss her forehead, but she veered her head away.

"No more stolen kisses, Elio."

I raised my hands in surrender and reluctantly left the room, heading for the nurses' station.

"Hello," the blonde nurse greeted.

I leaned against the counter. "How much do you make working here?"

She blinked, shocked by my question. "Huh?"

I held her gaze. "How much do you make?"

"Sir, that's none of your bus—"

"I'll pay you double to keep me informed of the patient in Room 12." I pointed at Cora's closed door.

"I can't do that, sir."

I reached into my pocket, removed a few hundred-dollar bills, and slid them along the counter. "There's more if you can be discreet."

She bit her lip and glanced around before reaching for the money. "I'm working tomorrow, and then I'm off for two days."

"That's fine. Keep me updated." I winked and turned to head back to the waiting area.

"How is she?" Savio asked.

"Pissed that I showed up."

"Give her space. She'll come around," he advised.

"I paid the nurse to keep me updated," I said as we walked out of the emergency room toward my car.

Savio paused and glanced at me. "She's going to kill you for that."

I shrugged and climbed into the car. "She has no choice."

* * *

The private jet sat on the tarmac. I sipped on my second drink of the night while waiting for the doors to open. Frustrated, I checked the time on my watch. It was already midnight. I closed my eyes and mulled over the past two days.

Cora hadn't answered any of my calls. The nurse I'd paid off told me Cora had checked out the following day, and I thanked her with ten thousand dollars. My mother and Marilyn took Cora home, and she'd been avoiding me since.

Renato had discreetly taken some photos of her and sent them to me. Like me, he did what it took to keep his woman safe, even if it pissed her off. I kept someone on Cora at all times and demanded a run-down of her activities. People might call it possessive and obsessed, but someone had mugged her. I hadn't wanted to push her at the hospital after the car accident, but I intended to find out who had laid their hands on her. Even though she hated me, I had her best interests at heart, and no one touched what was mine.

"Sir, they've arrived," my guard informed me.

I nodded as the door opened, and my team came aboard with my guest.

"I can walk!" Cora snapped.

I turned my head to see Eunoë pushing Cora forward. I jumped up and stalked toward him, moving Cora behind me. I pulled my fist back, intending to plant it in his face.

Cora caught my arm. "EJ!"

"Never put your hands on her again," I hissed at Eunoë.

Cora tugged on my arm. "You kidnapped me!" she accused hotly.

I took her wrist and kissed the back of her hand. "Cora, calm down."

"No, take your hands off me."

"Sir, we're about to take off," the flight attendant informed me.

I lifted Cora around the waist, walking us toward the bedroom at the back of the plane. I tossed her on the bed, and she immediately jumped up. I locked the door, preventing her escape.

"You can't keep me here," Cora snapped, her eyes flashing with fury. She sat on the bed, drawing her knees up and leaning against the headboard.

Resting my knee on the bed, I wrapped my hand around her ankle and yanked her toward me. "Look at me, Cora," I demanded when she turned her head away.

She sucked in a breath. "No."

I tipped my head to the side. "Cora."

"We'll be taking off in a few minutes. Please remain in your seats," the pilot announced over the intercom.

"Where are you taking me?" A scowl engulfed Cora's face.

"New York."

She turned her head to face me. "I have to work, EJ. Take me back."

"Something has come up, and I need to handle it personally."

"Then go. Leave me here."

"How are you feeling?" I ignored her plea as I ran a hand up her arm.

She jerked away and stood again, heading for the door. I grasped her around the waist and drew her against my chest.

"If you won't release me, at least leave me alone to get some work done."

"Are you going to tell me about the mugging?"

She tensed at my question. "No, because you'll go on a warpath for no reason."

Cora moved away, and I let her go this time. She unlocked the door and walked out of the bedroom, taking a seat and buckling up.

I sat next to her. "You can't avoid talking to me."

The stewardess brought drinks, and Cora grabbed a bottle of water. "Try me."

I frowned and blew out a frustrated breath. Standing, I moved to the seat across from her to continue working.

An hour into the flight, I gazed over at Cora to see she'd dozed off. Unbuckling her belt, I picked her up and carried her back to the bedroom, laying her on the bed under the covers. Locking the door, I removed my shirt, pants, and shoes before climbing in beside her.

"Stop playing games, EJ," she sighed in her sleep. She wrapped her leg around my waist and snuggled close.

I kissed her forehead and contemplated how to get her to fall in love with me again as I waited for sleep.

* * *

The pilot announced we'd arrived over the intercom, but Cora and I were already awake and dressed. She'd avoided talking to me since waking in my arms, so I decided to give her space.

We disembarked and headed for the waiting car. As soon as the door closed, we took off to the hotel I'd booked for our stay.

"How long are we here for?"

I pulled my phone from my pocket and turned it on. "No more than two weeks."

"Two weeks!" she shrieked.

I removed my wallet as the car arrived at the Hilton Hotel. "Here's my credit card so you can go shopping while I have my meetings."

"Don't insult me, EJ. I don't want your money. I have a business to run."

"Your assistant can run things while you're gone." I climbed out of the car.

Cora stepped out and crossed her arms when I tried to reach for her hand. I checked us in, and the desk clerk handed me the keys.

"Does your mother know you kidnapped me?" Cora asked as we rode in the elevator with the security guard.

"Probably."

"You are so selfish."

The elevator dinged when we reached the penthouse suite. Our guard checked the room before we entered. The bellhop arrived with our bags, and I handed him a tip. Cora plopped down on the couch and picked up the phone.

"Who are you calling?" I questioned.

She tucked her feet underneath her. A challenge

gleamed in her eyes as she snapped, "My mother. Is that all right, sir?"

I smirked at her snide comment and finished talking with my guard regarding the meeting later. "She's not to leave this room without one of you."

Jason was one of my younger soldiers. "Yes, sir."

I texted my brothers to let them know we'd arrived.

"EJ, I need food and a computer to work."

"Think of this as a vacation."

She scrunched up her nose. I wanted to take her into the bedroom and kiss away her frown, but now wasn't the time."

"I have my iPad. You can use that for now."

"Thank you." Cora grabbed my briefcase and removed my iPad.

"Jason will stay with you while I meet with my cousin."

"So you fly me out of Chicago just to leave me here alone in New York?"

"It's only for a few hours, and then we can have dinner."

"I'd rather eat my eyeballs."

I laughed as I picked up my briefcase and laptop and headed for the door. "I've missed that sassiness beneath the sweet demeanor."

Cora's voice faded as I closed the door behind me. "Whatever, EJ."

My phone dinged with a new message as I climbed into the car. Freddie was driving and headed for my cousin's nightclub.

Renato: *How was the plane ride?*

Me: *Cora's still pissed.*

Renato: *That happens when you kidnap someone.*

I smirked.

Me: *You have experience in that realm.*

Renato: *Fuck you.*

Me: *We're almost at Giosuè's club.*

Renato: *Call me if you need me.*

Freddie pulled up in front of Cove nightclub. I climbed out, and the doorman escorted me inside to Giosuè's office.

"It's open," Giosuè said in his thick Italian accent at my knock.

I pushed the door open to see two half-dressed women sitting on either side of his desk. "Cousin, I expected you to be alone." I unbuttoned my jacket and took a seat in the chair.

Giosuè grinned, removing the cigar from his mouth and placing it in the ashtray. "I was stressed."

I placed my briefcase on his desk. "Tell me what's going on?"

He motioned for his girls to leave us alone. "I was approached with some unsettling news concerning our little friend Gallagher."

"What news?"

Giosuè's pupils flared with rage. "He had a visitor."

"Who?"

"Someone who might cause us trouble."

"He's under strict orders for no visitors."

Giosuè picked up a folder from his desk and passed it to me.

I opened it to see pictures of a man meeting with Gallagher. "Who is this?"

"Gallagher's attorney, Izan Vargas."

"Vargas Cartel," I murmured, flipping through multiple photos of their meeting. "What happened to the chief keeping me under wraps?"

Giosuè sat back and clasped his hands together. "The Chief conveniently ended up dead."

"Fuck!"

"The Vargas Cartel has a long reach."

I'd heard a few stories about the Vargas Cartel, but they pretty much stayed in Mexico and ran their business. We never crossed paths, but if they were in New York, that meant Chicago was next.

I examined the photos. "How long were the meetings?"

"No more than thirty minutes."

My throat dried at the realization. "Enough time to get information."

"I hate to start a war, but they're on my territory," Giosuè stated.

I sighed. "Savio needs to be informed."

"Whatever needs to be done, but I'm not losing money."

"How is the art world going for you?"

"Your sister-in-law is on time with every sale. I can't complain," Giosuè replied.

"Good. Let me research Vargas, and I'll get back to you."

We shook hands, and I let myself out. I dialed Savio's number as I headed back to the car.

"How did the meeting go with Giosuè?" Savio asked.

"Not good," I said, throwing the briefcase on the back-seat of the car and sliding into the passenger seat. "We might have a problem," I elaborated as Freddie started the car.

"Besides Gallagher?" Savio inquired.

"Do you know Izan Vargas?"

The line went silent. "He's the lawyer of the Vargas Cartel. I know all of our rivals."

"We might have a big problem if what Giosuè told me is true."

"Where does Izan fit in with Gallagher?" Savio asked.

"They met a few times."

"Does Renato know?"

"Not yet. You were my first call."

"Send me whatever you have, and I'll call you later," Savio said, ending the call before I could reply.

I repocketed my phone as we headed down Times Square to the hotel. As Freddie drove, my thoughts drifted back to the day Cora and I went our separate ways...

"I don't want you in my life," she said.

"Cora, baby, please understand my life is complicated."

"Don't call me that. I'm not your baby. You promised the Cartel would never come between us."

"We're too young right now, Cora. I want you to be happy and go to college."

"We made a pact never to let our families dictate our futures. I'll never trust you again."

"In time, you'll understand that my life is the Cartel."

"If you walk out of my life, make sure you stay gone forever."

"Cora, we can be friends."

"When I leave, I won't have time for friends."

"What are you saying?"

"I'm saying we'll never be together. You've broken my

heart. Do you expect me to be okay with a decision you made without talking to me first?"

"Boss." Freddie called my name, pulling me from my thoughts.

"Yeah?"

"We're back at the hotel."

"Thanks." I climbed out of the car and grabbed my briefcase, my thoughts still on the day I broke up with Cora.

I'd just turned twenty and was preparing to join the family business. Cora was about to head to college. My father wanted me to make a choice—the cartel or Cora. I'd picked the family business over the love of my life, and I'd regretted it every day since.

Chapter 3

Cora

EJ came into the room with a lost look. I asked him what was wrong, but he said nothing. He simply lifted me off the couch and kissed me long and hard until I was drowning in sensation.

"We can't be friends, Cora," he said, removing his jacket and tie.

Part of me wanted to question his sudden mood. He was the last man I'd had sex with. My friends had set me up on dates plenty of times, but I always compared them to Elio Calabresi, the arrogant, sexy, demanding, yet sweet man I'd learned to hate.

He carried me to the bed and hovered over me, his gaze intense. "Tell me no, Cora, because I won't let you go again."

I gazed into the eyes that spoke to my soul. "This is a one-time thing."

He smirked as he stripped off his clothes and quickly relieved me of mine.

My eyes moved down his chiseled body. "I'm serious, EJ—"

I was cut off when he claimed my mouth and plunged his tongue inside. Against all logic, I melted into him. I cupped the back of his neck and sucked on his tongue. He moved down my body, licking and nibbling until he reached my core. I watched him slowly spread my legs. My pussy throbbed, and my heart pounded as EJ dove in, rolling his tongue between my slick folds. The man I hated for breaking my heart years ago was the only man who could give me this kind of pleasure.

"EJ, please," I pleaded when his finger slipped in and out of my soaking center.

My right leg was cocked up on the bed. My pleading did nothing to get him to show me mercy.

Slap!

"Mmm... yes," I cooed, cupping the back of his neck as he slapped my thigh.

Slap!

"So wet for me." EJ slapped my pussy lips before giving them a gentle kiss to ease the sting.

He crawled up my body, hooked my leg around his waist, and eased his thick length inside me. His thrusts were deep and firm, driving me crazy. He suckled my breasts, swirling his tongue around each nipple as he rocked against me.

"Fuck! I missed you," EJ groaned, wrapping a hand around my throat and brushing his finger across my bottom lip.

"Ummmm." I moaned and arched off the bed.

"Damn," Elio grunted.

He pulled out and lifted my legs over his shoulders before plunging back inside me. This six-foot, two-hundred-pound man was dominating me, and I loved it.

I fisted the sheets as his body pummeled mine. "Yes! Elio, please."

With a growl, he flipped us so I was straddling him. I rolled my hips as I rode him, our hands interlocked above his head, my long hair teasing his face.

"Cora... ah, shit," he huffed.

I lifted, holding the tip of his dick at my entrance.

"Stop playing," he growled.

I smiled as I slid back down his dick, grinding against his upward thrusts.

"Oh, God, EJ!" I shouted as I bounced up and down on his thick cock.

"Fuck! I love you, Cora," he groaned as we both came.

I fell on top of him, trying to catch my breath. He peppered kisses over my forehead and hair as I dozed off in his arms.

* * *

I woke up in an empty bed. I slowly turned onto my back, staring at the ceiling. The sun beamed through the window, and I groaned at the brightness as I climbed out of bed. I sauntered to the bathroom and looked at myself in the mirror. Last night shouldn't have happened.

An hour later, I emerged from the bathroom refreshed. I dressed in a long maxi dress that highlighted my toned frame. Mckayla, Savio's wife, got me into yoga and Pilates when I didn't have time to join a gym.

Outside the Calabresi family, I mostly hung out with Mckayla and loved babysitting the kids. The Calibresis were like family. I thought EJ was gorgeous when we first met, and he only became more so as we got older. My mom worked for his family, so I was always around him and his brothers, who regarded me as a little sister.

But they had no clue about my secret. EJ would hate that I'd never told him, but I thought it was too much to put on him when he was so immersed in his family's business. Only my mom knew of my miscarriage when I was nineteen. She never judged me and encouraged me to focus on achieving my dreams and goals. I put everything on the back burner and studied hard at college so I could open my own business.

"Miss Cora," Freddie called from the other side of the bedroom door.

I unlocked it. "Yes?"

"Mr. Calabresi had a meeting, but he wanted me to ensure you had room service."

"Thank you. I'll get something later. Are you able to take me shopping?" I knew this would be my chance to get back to Chicago if I could ditch Freddie.

"Yes, ma'am."

"Thanks. Give me five minutes, and we can go."

"No problem."

"Oh, did Mr. Calabresi say how long he'd be?"

"No, I'm afraid not."

I shut the door and looked around the empty room. This was the last time I'd let EJ force his way into my life. At twenty-seven, I had plans and a business to run. I wouldn't put my life on hold again because he'd now decided he wanted something he couldn't give me years ago. I was no longer a naive teenager who hung on his every word.

My father's death and my miscarriage put a lot of things into perspective, like how short life was. My happiness was my priority from now on.

I stepped out of the hotel and slid into the back of the waiting car. Freddie shut my door and approached the passenger side as Jason started the car. We pulled off and drove toward Saks. I had no phone to call my mom or friends, and they were probably worried about me.

"What time is it?"

Freddie checked his watch. "Noon."

"Great, can I use your phone?"

Freddie frowned. "I was advised against that, Miss Cora."

"Freddie, we've known each other for a while. I just want to call my mom."

He sighed. "Mr. Calabresi will kill me."

"I promise not to say anything," I pleaded with my hands in prayer position.

Freddie looked from me to Jason and back again before reaching into his pocket and dialing a number on speaker.

"Is something wrong?" I heard EJ ask.

I was suddenly reminded of his harsh groans as we'd had sex.

"Miss Cora would like to call her mother."

"Did you sleep well, Cora?" EJ questioned.

I didn't answer.

"Are you still ignoring me?" he asked as we arrived at Saks. "Cora?"

I ignored him again and looked at Freddie. "Can we go, please?"

"Cora, don't be mad," EJ cajoled.

"Goodbye, EJ." I ended the call.

Freddie opened the door and helped me out. I was already planning a distraction so I could escape and return home.

As I headed to the dress section, I accidentally bumped into a hard body. "Oh, I'm so sorry."

Coal-black eyes surveyed me. The man I'd collided with smiled, and the dimples in his cheeks alone would have most women falling at his feet. "No problem at all, beautiful."

"Miss Cora, is everything all right?" Freddie asked, his eyes watchful.

I cleared my throat. "I'm fine, Freddie."

With another twitch of his lips, the man walked off, followed by an entourage of men. Who was he to have five men guarding him?

I shrugged and continued to the dress section. Grabbing a few items, I turned to find Freddie at the door. "Freddie, can I have some privacy, please?"

Freddie frowned. "My job is to stay with you at all times."

"Can you stand outside the store? I can't go anywhere. I'm only trying on these dresses in the changing room. Nothing will happen to me there." I gave him a reassuring smile.

Freddie nodded reluctantly and remained where he was as I walked off. I liked Freddie, but sometimes, having guards around the clock was suffocating.

I placed both dresses on the back of the changing room door and looked around to see if anyone else was there.

"This dress is too tight," I heard a woman say.

I knocked on the door next to me and waited for her to come out.

"Yes, can I help you?" Her brows furrowed in confusion.

"Hi, um, I need a huge favor."

"I don't have any money."

"No, that's not the problem. My friend is waiting for me, but I can't get out of here without those two men up front following me."

"Why don't you call the police?" she asked.

"Usually, I would, but I don't have a phone. Everything was stolen when my apartment was broken into."

"Who are they?"

"My boyfriend's bodyguards. He cheated on me but thinks I'm still his property."

Her eyes softened. "I'm sorry, honey. I hate cheaters."

"Can I use your phone to call a cab?"

"Sure." She reached into her bag and handed me her phone.

Tomorrow, I might have regrets. EJ could burn the city down searching for me, but I needed space from what had happened between us.

"Are you leaving now?" I asked the lady.

"I am. What can I do to help?"

"I need a distraction."

"Leave it to me."

I quickly organized an Uber and kept out of sight as the woman headed toward one of the sales reps. I didn't know what she said, but a grim look came across the sales rep's face. She stomped over to Freddie and started yelling at him. Jason intervened, and I took my chance to slip out. I quickly left the store and hurried to the Uber I'd ordered.

"Yes. To the airport, please." I slammed the door, and the car took off.

I released a breath and held onto the phone I'd taken from the woman. I dialed my mom's number and waited for it to ring.

"Hello?"

"Mom?"

"Cora! Where are you?"

My heart did cartwheels at hearing her voice. "I'll explain later. If anyone asks, you haven't heard from me."

"Like who?"

"Anyone. Especially EJ."

"What's happened, Cora?"

My chest was tight with panic. I didn't want her to see EJ in a bad light, but she had to know about his antics. "He brought me to New York."

"Oh, dear, that boy," Mom groaned.

"Yeah, he kidnapped me."

The Uber driver glanced at me curiously in the rearview mirror.

"He's lost his mind, and I'm done with his hot and cold behavior."

"I'll be his first call once he finds out," Mom pointed out.

"Block him. I told him to leave me alone."

"Call me when you're home safe."

I ended the call and stared out the window. I needed a life outside of the Calabresi family. I'd never find real love if I constantly let EJ dictate my emotions.

"Here we are. JFK airport," the driver announced.

"Thanks." I gave him a large tip.

Heading into the terminal, I turned off the phone and dropped it in the trash.

* * *

The next flight to Chicago wasn't until ten p.m., so I spent the next few hours keeping a low profile in case anyone from the Calabresi Cartel was looking for me. I was relieved to board my flight and hailed a cab once I landed in Chicago. I was exhausted and ready for bed, but I knew EJ would have men at my place, so I decided to go to one of my best friend's houses.

I knocked on the door and waited. It was almost midnight, so she was probably in bed.

"Cora?" Anissa asked groggily as she answered the door. Anissa lived in Northfield and was dating a nurse.

"Hi, Anissa. Sorry to bug you, but I need a place to crash for a few days."

"Come inside." Anissa moved aside so I could enter.

Like me, she ran a business, a bakery. All her life, she'd loved to bake cookies and desserts. We even looked a little alike. We were the same height, and both had auburn hair and an athletic build.

"Thanks. I know it's late."

She shut the door behind me. "What's wrong with your place?"

I sighed as I sat on the couch. "EJ."

She frowned at the mention of his name and sat beside me. "What happened this time?"

"It's a long story I don't want to get into tonight." I ran a hand over my face and yawned. "Can we talk in the morning?"

"Sure. You know where the guest bedroom is."

"Is Mitchel here?" I asked as I stood. I didn't want to interrupt anything.

"No, he had to work in the emergency room tonight."

I pushed open the door of the guest bedroom. "Thanks again, Anissa."

"You're welcome, but you're spilling the beans tomorrow. I need details." She grinned and wagged her finger at me before disappearing into her room.

I lay on the bed and toed off my shoes. I'd call my mom tomorrow. I was exhausted from the trip.

After brushing my teeth, I crawled under the covers, my mind full of memories...

"I like you, Cora."

"You may like me, EJ, but you still flirted with those girls in front of my face." I kicked my feet in the pool.

EJ's mother, Adelina, was hosting a party for his eighteenth birthday and had invited a few friends over. I was in a one-piece bathing suit, but most of the other girls wore string bikinis. Every girl on the block wanted a Calabresi brother, and sometimes, my jealousy got the better of me.

EJ clipped my chin, pulling me close to peck me on the lips. "No one else matters but you."

"Really?"

"Yes. What do I have to do to prove it?"

"Apply to college."

He looked annoyed at my statement, but instead of the angry retort I expected, he grabbed me, sprinted to the pool, and jumped in.

"Elio Jr, I'm going to kill you!" I shouted, smoothing my hair down.

He laughed. "You'll have to catch me first." He swam to the other side of the pool, climbed out, and ran away.

I was pissed that my hair was messed up and spent the rest of the day ignoring him.

Chapter 4

Elio Jr

My frustration was at an all-time high, and Cora skipping out on me yesterday only made things worse. I'd been with my cousin, trying to get more information on the Vargas Cartel, when Freddie called to inform me that Cora had ditched him at the mall. I'd tried to call her a hundred times since, to no avail. Cora knew I hated to be ignored.

I wanted to call and check on Cora again as Freddie drove me to the jail where Gallagher was being held, but I decided to give her space for now. Once I returned to Chicago, I wouldn't let up until she agreed to be mine.

We reached the prison, and Freddie parked the car. The cops on the Calabresi payroll had allowed me to visit with Gallagher for a few minutes. I was escorted to the meeting room, where I sat and waited. I placed my brief-case on the floor as the guards walked in with Gallagher in chains. His expression was a hard grimace as they motioned for him to sit and secured his hands and feet.

Gallagher and I stared at each other.

"You know why I'm here," I muttered.

His suspicious gaze moved from me to the guards.

I lifted the briefcase and pulled out the folder, removing the photo and pushing it toward him. "Why were you meeting with Izan Vargas?"

Gallagher glanced at the photo. "He's my lawyer."

"You don't have a lawyer." I leaned forward with my hands clasped on the table, pinning him with my gaze. "Why was Izan Vargas here?"

He grinned. "That question will be answered in good time."

"Vargas can't protect you."

"I know, but at least I won't be alone in hell when they take your family out," he growled.

"Just remember you started this fight." I picked up the picture and tossed it back in my briefcase. I stood and nodded to the guard.

Gallagher's eyes narrowed, and fear crept into his expression as he looked at the guards. "You can't do this."

"I haven't done anything yet, Agent Gallagher."

"Wait!" he shouted.

I opened the door. "You've had plenty of chances."

"No! Don't do this to me!"

I shut the door on his screams and cries for help.

I reached into my pocket as my phone rang to see Savio's name on the screen. I'd call him back once I was out of the prison. As I walked, I saw a familiar man. I kept my eyes forward and my expression blank as I moved past him. What the fuck was Izan Vargas doing here?

Freddie and Jason were waiting in the car as I emerged from the prison. I climbed in and motioned for them to leave, pulling my phone from my pocket and calling Savio.

"We got word that the Vargas Cartel is planning to start a war," Savio informed me immediately.

"Why?"

"My sources say Gallagher fed them some intel, but they intended to come after us for a while."

"Damn it."

"When are you back?"

"I'll call the pilot to get the plane ready."

"Good. We need to have a meeting and figure out their moves."

"I saw Izan at the prison," I tell him.

"Did he say anything to you?"

"No, and that tells me his family is already in Chicago."

"I'll ensure the family has double security," Savio said.

"You know the girls will hate that," I replied.

"No choice with this new information. Gallagher probably gave them everything down to the favorite places we like to shop."

I pinched the bridge of my nose. As the family lawyer, I had to keep my distance in certain situations, but Enrique Vargas sending his brother Izan to talk to Gallagher heightened my stress level.

"I'm heading back to Chicago," I informed Savio.

"Meet me first thing in the morning."

I clenched my jaw. "I have something else I need to handle."

"It can wait, EJ."

"It's Cora."

Savio went silent. I knew that ignoring his request would put us at odds.

"Handle it after this meeting. I'm not asking," he

instructed. This was the Don speaking, not my brother. But Cora meant the same to me as his wife, Mckayla, did to him.

I ended the call as Jason arrived at the airport. I skimmed over my text thread to see how Cora was when a notification with Gallagher's name appeared. The link opened a video clip as soon as I clicked on it.

"Breaking news. The death of FBI Agent Cade Gallagher has raised questions about the security measures in place in the prison. We'll have more details tonight at seven."

I slipped the phone into my pocket and sat back, wondering what the Vargas Cartel was going to do next.

* * *

My brothers Savio, Sante, and Renato were seated around the table with the other bosses as I entered the meeting. I took a seat and placed the briefcase on top of the conference table.

Savio leaned forward and made eye contact with everyone. "Enrique Vargas is in town."

One of the cartel bosses sat up straight. "When did this happen?"

"I went to New York to handle Cade Gallagher and discovered that Izan Vargas is his lawyer," I explained. I opened the briefcase and removed the photos, spreading them on the desk so everyone could see them.

"Why are we only learning this now, Savio?" Alvize asked, glaring at my brother.

Savio had taken care of Greco, Costa, and any other enemies who had tried to destroy our family. Having the mayor on our side worked in our favor, but Alvize still worried that the other shoe would drop. I didn't blame him. We were in a situation we didn't ask for.

"I don't need to run anything through you until I consider it worth discussing. And that time is now," Savio replied coolly.

Alvize and my brother glared at each other.

"Do we know why Enrique Vargas and his family are here?" another boss questioned.

Savio replied, "No word yet, but I'll find out."

"I don't like this one bit," Vincenzo responded.

"I'll keep an eye on them for now and request a meeting," Savio said.

Shocked voices murmured around him.

"If we do that, it'll look weak," Bera objected.

"My family is far from weak," Renato spat.

Bera knew better than to question the Don.

"All I'm saying is that Vargas is dangerous and doesn't follow the rules of a traditional Cartel," Bera stated.

"Enrique Vargas isn't stupid." I didn't take threats to my family lightly, and Enrique would die today if I agreed with my brothers. My father taught us to protect the family at all costs.

"EJ will set up a meeting to find out why he's here," Savio explained.

The phone on the table rang, and all eyes locked on it, wondering who could access the number at our private conference.

Sante leaned forward and hit the answer button.

"Mr. Calabresi?" his secretary asked.

"Yes."

"I have Mr. Vargas on the line," Andrea said, causing silence to descend on the room.

"Put him through."

"Sorry it took me a while to make my presence known." A thick accent spoke through the phone.

"How did you get this number?" Savio demanded.

The man chuckled. "Am I speaking with Don Savio Calabresi?"

"You are. How can I assist you, Mr. Vargas?" Savio asked patiently.

"Can I assume that Sante and Renato are with you?"

I frowned. His question raised red flags.

"My brothers' whereabouts don't concern you."

"Protective. I like that. I'm the same with my brother, Izan," Enrique said.

"How can I help you, Mr. Vargas?" Savio repeated.

"I'll be in touch soon." The line went dead.

"He's trying to plant himself in control," I said, looking at my brothers.

Renato leaned back in the chair with a smug smirk. "No one controls me."

"I want everyone to increase your security and tighten up your import and export orders," Savio instructed the occupants of the room before dismissing them.

Everybody filed out except my brothers and me.

"Father needs to know that Vargas is in town," Vincenzo said.

Savio rubbed his beard. "Not yet."

"The sooner, the better," I agreed with my little brother.

Savio sighed and rose from his chair. "Fine, we can go now."

Renato looked at me. "I'll ride with you."

He followed me to the car while Savio, Sante, and Vincenzo rode together.

Renato studied me thoughtfully as we headed toward

our parents' house. "Your expression tells me you're pissed about more than Enrique Vargas."

"Cora hasn't answered my calls."

"She's a woman. They get pissed and ignore us."

"Sonya didn't ignore you," I pointed out.

"She had no choice because I kidnapped her." Renato smirked at me.

"I tried that with Cora, and it didn't end well."

"Little brother, you know Cora won't make it easy for you."

I rubbed my temples. "I hurt her badly."

"You were a kid," Renato reasoned.

"Yeah, but she refuses to hear me out."

"Make her listen." Renato's phone rang, and he grabbed it from his pocket,

I tried to think of anything besides my problems as Renato spoke with his wife, Sonya.

Freddie navigated the construction work at my parents' estate and parked in front of the garage. I jogged up the stairs and opened the door as Savio's limo pulled up.

Marilyn greeted me, and I kissed her on the cheek.

"Are you mad at me too?" I asked, seeing her glare.

"I regard you as a son, EJ, but if you hurt Cora again, you and I will have a problem."

"Marilyn, you know Cora is stubborn and refuses to let me explain."

"She's worked hard to be independent of this family after what happened," Marilyn exclaimed.

"We were young and—"

"That's no excuse when you had—" Marilyn caught herself and pressed her lips together.

I opened my mouth to question her when my mother came around the corner with my nephew, SJ, behind her.

Mother clapped her hands excitedly. "All my boys are home! Are you staying for dinner?"

I kissed her cheek and ruffled my nephew's hair as he ran to his father. Savio grinned as he lifted him in the air.

"Where's Pop?" Renato joined the conversation.

"In the pool with the kids." Mother pointed to the backyard.

"Has Cora come by?" I asked.

My mother and Marilyn glanced at each other.

Mother answered, "No."

"She's usually here for lunch during a break from work," I said.

"Are you hungry?" Mother asked, changing the subject.

"No."

"Elio, we can worry about that later," Sante stated.

I left the conversation alone and went to the back-yard. My father sat near the pool, laughing at the kids as they splashed in the water. Rena and Mckayla weren't around, which meant my parents were on babysitting duty.

My father stood to hug me.

"We need to talk," I said.

He didn't respond, walking over to pick up his cigar before sitting under the cabana.

"The Vargas Cartel is in town." I looked directly at him and waited for a response.

"Enrique Vargas called us today," Savio added.

The man I was named after blew out cigar smoke as he listened. He probably wanted more information before giving his opinion. Unless he was needed, he let Savio handle everything now that he was retired. We appreciated him allowing us to make decisions and mistakes without trying to take over.

"The Vargas and Calabresi Cartels have a past I do not wish to repeat," Father said, scanning our faces. "Enrique's father, Amadias, ran his family without an ounce of respect for anyone. He killed women and children, and he stole money from our family. He wanted to expand, and we refused. Eventually, a truce was made, but Amadias decided not to honor it and is no longer living." Father laid out all the things I knew would spark a war.

"So Enrique came to Chicago to take over." Renato folded his arms over his chest.

Father placed the cigar on the tray. "I would advise you to see what he wants, but be cautious."

Savio nodded in understanding.

"Calabresis don't negotiate," Renato spat.

"It's not about negotiating, son. I'll do anything to protect our family, but I won't put your mother through another war. Enrique must want something. Find out what."

"Whatever he wants is irrelevant," I hissed, on the same page as Renato. Enrique Vargas needed to know we couldn't be intimidated.

"I can set up a meeting," Sante suggested.

"Good. Savio, as the Don, you need to be ready to put a deal in motion if it comes to that to keep the peace."

"We don't sell out!" Renato barked, startling the kids.

"Lower your voice," Father said, pinning Renato with a stern gaze.

"Enrique made the first move. I'll do some more investigating," I said.

"Is that agent handled in New York?" Father questioned.

I nodded. "No longer a concern."

My brothers decided to hang with the kids, and I left with a grumbling stomach to find something to eat in the kitchen. I paused outside my father's office when I heard low murmurs within.

"She's still hurt," Mother said.

"I know. I wish she'd told him years ago," Marilyn replied.

"I'm upset she didn't say anything, but I understand."

My brows knitted in confusion. Who were they talking about? I entered the room to see my mother and Marilyn huddled together.

"EJ!" Mother removed her arm from around Marilyn.

My gaze darted between them. "What's the matter?"

"Nothing." Marilyn wiped the tears from her eyes.

"Is it Cora?"

"Honey, no. You need to stop worrying about Cora and focus on meeting someone new," Mother advised.

"I'm hungry. Did you cook, Marilyn?" I asked, ignoring my mother's "advice."

"I-I did," Marilyn stuttered.

"Marilyn's famous lobster and beef Wellington." Mother hooked her arm through mine and walked me out of my father's office.

I made a note to talk to Marilyn about whatever they were discussing later after I found Cora.

Chapter 5

Cora

"He'll be fine. Give him the medicine with his food." I rubbed the chocolate pug's head and smiled.

His owner had brought him in when she noticed he wasn't eating like usual. I filled out the forms and motioned for my assistant to finish them, leaving the examination room and walking down the hall to my office. No sooner had I taken a seat when there was a knock at the door. I looked up to see Anissa carrying two bags in her hands.

I waved her to come in. "I thought you were at work?"

Anissa placed the bags on my desk and removed the burgers and fries, passing one to me. "I figured since you skipped breakfast this morning, we could catch up for lunch."

"In other words, Mitchel worked through lunch."

A flip of her middle finger made me laugh.

Anissa sat in the chair on the other side of my desk.

"So, tell me what happened. You turn up on my doorstep in the middle of the night after going AWOL."

"EJ kidnapped me."

"Kidnapped you!" Anissa leaped out of her seat.

I shushed her and quickly closed my office door. "Calm down before the whole office knows."

Anissa stared at me. "Cora, you're not making sense."

I unwrapped my cheeseburger. "He was upset that I went on a date during the holidays."

Anissa shook her head. "Are we talking about the same EJ who flew you and your friends to Vegas for your twenty-first birthday and paid for your home?"

"Don't remind me. I've tried to pay him back, but he refuses to take my money."

Anissa supported my dating but knew that EJ and I had a history. I'd tried to move on, but no one held my heart like he did.

"Because he wants you indebted to him." Anissa tossed a French fry in her mouth.

"I skipped out on him in New York."

"Did you sleep with him?"

I choked on my drink and patted my chest.

Anissa sipped on her smoothie. "That's a yes. I hope you used protection."

Anissa knew about my miscarriage when I was younger.

"We were too caught up in the moment, but I'm on birth control."

"I'm glad you had a little fun. I want you to be happy."

"I am happy."

"Not if you're only working and hanging out with Devi and me." Anissa's lips bunched together in a pout.

I was offended by her statement and threw a balled-up napkin at her. "My best friend doesn't like me anymore."

She laughed and tossed the napkin back at me. "I want you to be happy, and that doesn't mean putting your life on hold."

"I go on dates."

"When?"

"All the time."

"You've had two dates in the last year, Cora."

"I'm busy." I dropped the bags of food in the waste basket and grabbed my paperwork for my next appointment.

Anissa stood and picked up her purse to leave. "Never too busy for love. Call me when you make it home, and we can set up a girl's weekend."

We hugged, and I led her out of my office. I wasn't looking where I was going and bumped into a large body.

"Oh, so sorry." I stepped back, and Anissa plowed into me. I looked from the bulldog on the leash into dark brown eyes.

"No, my apologies," the man said in a thick accent.

"Who do we have here?" I bent to rub the bulldog's head, and she licked my hand.

"My little princess," he replied and lifted her.

Anissa cleared her throat and nudged my shoulder.

I elbowed her in the stomach and smiled at the man. "Is there something I can help you with?"

"Princess hasn't eaten for two days."

I nodded and motioned for him to follow me up to the front. "What's your name?"

"Enrique."

I lifted our schedule booklet for the day and noticed

his name wasn't written down. "We don't have you booked in, but since it's slow, I could check her out."

"Thank you, Cora."

"How do you know my name?"

He motioned at my name badge on my white coat.

I smacked my forehead. "Brain fart."

"Cora, I have to go. I'll leave you to it." Anissa smirked.

"We should have dinner soon and catch up."

Anissa hugged me again and whispered in my ear. "Sexy and tall with an amazing accent. Grab condoms." With that, she waved goodbye and disappeared.

"Excuse my friend."

Enrique grinned. "She's funny."

"Please tell me you didn't hear that."

He made a zipping motion across his lips, and I groaned in embarrassment.

"Let's get Princess to the exam room," I said, striving to remain professional.

The door opened again as we were heading to the examination room, and I paused as I saw a delivery guy holding a bunch of flowers.

"Delivery for Cora Sica," he said, holding the bouquet.

I waved for him to place them on the counter. "That's me."

"Sign here," the delivery guy said.

"Secret admirer?" Enrique asked.

I picked up the card and read the inscription. *You're all I think about.* "No, an ex who doesn't know how to leave me alone." EJ must be back in Chicago. "Julia, can you put these in water and place them in my office?"

Julia replied, "You got it, Cora."

I checked my watch and saw it was time for my next appointment, but I still had to take care of Princess.

"Julia will have you fill out some paperwork while I look over Princess," I told Enrique.

He hitched a thumb toward his dog. "I'd like to stay with her. She's like a child."

"Sure. Come with me." I walked down the hall to the examination room and opened the door for him to enter.

He lifted Princess onto the table. "How long have you done this work?"

"Four years."

Enrique laced his hands in front of him. "If you don't mind me asking, are you married?"

I checked Princess's eyes and ears. "Single." I wiggled my hand in the air and then rubbed Princess's stomach. She licked my hand again.

"Princess likes you."

"She's a good girl," I cooed.

"Have dinner with me."

I looked up in surprise."

"You're a beautiful woman, Cora."

I shook my head. "I'm sorry. I can't."

He walked around the examination table to face me. "Boyfriend?"

"No."

"No husband. No boyfriend. I have a crazy ex."

He placed a hand on top of mine. "Nothing scares me, *hermosa*."

"Um, I should finish the examination." I removed my hand and picked up the chart to take notes on Princess.

We were interrupted by a knock at the door, and I opened it to see Julia holding a piece of paper. "Sorry to interrupt, but a gentleman just stopped by and said he'd like to buy the building."

"This is the second time. He needs to take a hint." I grabbed the card from Julia's hand and tossed it in the trash.

"Business troubles?" Enrique asked.

"Some guy wants to buy my clinic. I have a pretty good idea why."

Enrique glanced around the room. "It's a small clinic. You get much traffic?"

"I do okay, but better would be nice." I wrapped up my notes on Princess and passed them to Julia to add to the computer system.

"The neighborhood's not the most exciting."

"Yeah. I wanted a place accessible to everyone, no matter their finances. Princess is all set to go home. Julia will give you the notes and advise encouraging her to eat."

Enrique lifted Princess off the table, and we left the room.

"Have dinner with me," Enrique repeated.

"You don't give up, do you?" I looked at him.

"Not when it's a beautiful woman."

"Nice to meet you, Princess. You too, Enrique." I stuck my hand out for him to shake.

He lifted it to his lips, kissing the back of my hand. "Maybe I'll have two princesses in my life."

I shook my head and watched Julia check him out before returning to my office to finish some paperwork.

* * *

"You've reached Elio Calabresi Jr. Please leave a message."

The same message repeated. I knew EJ would be screening my calls to teach me a lesson for ignoring him. It was childish, but that was how EJ handled things when they didn't go the way he wanted.

I drank the rest of my wine and curled up on the couch, watching Love Story for the millionth time. Work had been busy, so I came home, took a long bath, and popped the leftovers from last night in the oven.

My phone rang, and I lifted it to see my mom's name on the screen. "Hi, Mom," I answered with a smile.

"She remembers her mother," Mom teased.

"Sorry. I forgot to call you when I got back."

"Adelina wants you to come over to the house."

"When?"

"Now. Family dinner."

"I can't. I'm slammed with work."

"Cora, you've missed the last three family dinners," Mom pointed out.

I sighed. It seemed my time of ignoring the Calabresi family was over. I'd wanted to distance myself, but it had only made things more complicated and put a wedge between EJ's parents and me. "Okay. I'll be there."

"Good. A driver is outside."

"Is EJ there?"

"No."

"Mom!"

"He's on his way, Cora."

I groaned, listening to Mom describe what she'd cooked for dinner as I stood and turned the movie off.

The doorbell rang. "Mom, I have to go. I'll see you soon."

Ending the call, I went to open the front door. "Hi, Freddie."

Freddie's expression settled into a frown. "Cora."

"Are you still mad about New York?"

"No." Freddie stepped inside and closed the door behind him. "Just means I need to keep an even closer eye on you."

"My life is none of EJ's business." I poked Freddie in the chest.

He lifted his hands placatingly. "He only wants to talk."

I shook my head in disbelief. "He kidnapped me! I'm not falling for his lies anymore. Take me to this dinner and back, Freddie. Don't try to take me anywhere else, or I swear I'll call the police."

I pushed my feet into my sandals and pulled my hair into a bun. Grabbing my purse, I paused by the door. "Is he in the car?"

"No."

I relaxed and locked my door, following Freddie to the elevator.

* * *

The thirty-minute drive gave me time to clear my head. I wouldn't engage with EJ if he tried to start an argument. My goal was to catch up with his mother and father, then return home and prepare for work the next day.

Freddie parked in front of the house before climbing out and opening my door. I approached the house to see Adelina waiting for me with her hands on her hips.

I felt like a fourteen-year-old again. "Hi, Adelina."

"Is that all I get, *mi amore*?" Adelina extended her arms and pulled me into a tight hug. She drew back and linked our hands together. "That's better. Let me look at you."

"You're acting like it's been years." I laughed.

SJ came barreling down the hallway and stretched out his arms. I picked him up and hugged him.

"*Ragazzino*, you're too heavy for Cora to pick you up." Mckayla appeared and took him from my arms.

"I'm not that heavy, Mommy." Savio Jr. laughed at his mom and poked his lips out for a kiss.

"Come in and see everybody." Adelina interlocked her arm with mine and led me to the living room, where the kids and Vincenzo were playing. "Look who finally showed up." Adelina beamed.

I waved to the kids.

"Where have you been, Cora?" Rena pushed a Monopoly toy around the board.

"Working."

"Come help in the kitchen, Rena," Adelina demanded, pulling me along.

"Who's coming for dinner?" I asked.

"Just family." Adelina released me.

Mom was in the kitchen, and I hugged her before stealing a piece of the celery she was chopping. "Where's Elio Sr.?"

"Working in his office, even though he's retired," Adelina muttered.

I giggled at her annoyance with her husband.

"So, spill the beans." Rena sat next to me on the stool.

"Nothing to spill."

"EJ almost killed a guy on Christmas Eve."

"What do you expect? He's a Calabresi."

Rena chortled as Adelina's brows drew together.

"We know EJ took you to New York, and you left

him." Mckayla stepped up to the counter and picked up a piece of chicken, taking a bite. "We've all had our share of Calabresi men doing something crazy."

I sighed. "He wanted to talk, and I wasn't interested."

"How much longer are you going to hide from him?" Mom asked.

"I'd like to know the answer to that question," EJ said, appearing behind me.

Chapter 6

Elio Jr

All eyes except Cora's were on me. Instead, she pulled out her phone and pretended to scroll through her messages. She'd ignored all my calls and the flowers I'd had delivered to apologize for New York.

Savio wanted more information on the Vargas brothers and set a meeting to make sure all parties understood that no blood should be shed. Cora forced me to act up when she got this way. I promised never to put our business before family and friends, but ignoring me was the last straw.

A chill ran through the room. "Cora."

"Not now, EJ."

"You ignored my calls."

"EJ," Mother interrupted.

I shook my head, indicating she should stay out of things. "If Cora can ditch her bodyguards and worry everyone, she's capable of speaking for herself."

Cora swiveled in her seat, her nostrils flared and her

eyes shooting daggers at me. Cora was always reserved and calm in front of the family, but I knew how to push her buttons to get a reaction.

"EJ, come and talk to me in the other room." Mother removed her apron and pulled me out of the kitchen. "I raised you better than this," she hissed once we were in the dining room.

"Madre, you don't understand—"

She raised her hand to stop me. "You have no authority over Cora. I want you to apologize and leave her alone."

"No."

"That wasn't a request."

"She's behaving childishly." My blood boiled at being ignored.

"If you want any chance with her, you need to back off and let her decide when she's ready to talk."

I frowned. "She's not the only one who was hurt."

"EJ, as my son, I will always have your back, but what you did was wrong. Sending Freddie to put her on a plane without letting her mother or me know." Mother chided me for my arrogance.

"Pops would do the same if it came to you."

She smiled. "He would, and I'd give him a piece of my mind." She drew me in close for a hug. "Come and sit so we can eat."

"I promise to behave for dinner."

Mother cupped my chin. "Thank you."

"Did she tell you about the robbery?"

"No, but tonight we leave it alone, son."

The women and kids piled into the dining room with the food. Savio and Sante arrived, and Pops slipped in behind my mother. He kissed her on the cheek and took his seat at the head of the table. Renato sat next to his wife.

I grabbed Cora's hand as she went to sit next to Mckayla. She tried to snatch it away, but I tugged her into the seat beside me.

Cora yanked her hand out of my hold and turned her attention to my mother and father.

I stretched my arm along the back of her chair and leaned in close. "Playing games will get you punished."

"Marilyn's dinner looks wonderful," Mckayla said as Marilyn placed the baked chicken on the table.

"Cora finally came, so we wanted to celebrate." Marilyn squeezed her daughter's hand.

Laughter and conversation spread around the table, but I only wanted Cora's attention on me. It was time she came home and realized we were meant to be together.

"EJ, how is business going?" Pop wiped his mouth with the napkin.

"Great, nothing to concern the board about. We're keeping an eye on things."

"What's going on with your business, Cora?" Mckayla asked.

"No business talk tonight." Mother hushed.

"Some people are trying to step on our toes," I blurted.

"Not tonight, EJ!" Mother fussed.

"Since we can't talk about business, let's discuss Cora's accident." Renato gulped his water.

Cora glared at Renato, and he winked. She hunched her shoulders. "Nothing to tell."

"Someone tried to rob you." Pops frowned.

"Yes, Mr. Calabresi, but I'm fine," Cora answered.

"Until we catch them, you're not fine," I said, draining my glass of cognac.

Cora shifted in her seat. "The police will handle my case."

"Cora, you're one of us. We can handle it way better," Renato commented.

"Not in front of the kids, Renato," Sonya groaned.

I nodded. "Renato's right. Until they're caught, you'll need to be watched."

"Once again, you're trying to barge into my life." Cora's frustration was clear as she dropped the napkin on the table and jumped out of her chair.

"Cora." Marilyn stood and tried to calm her down.

"No. He's pigheaded and rude. I don't need your help." Cora stormed out of the room.I chased after her, following her up to the guest room she used when she stayed over.

She paced back and forth in front of the window. "EJ, I want you to leave me alone."

"Give me one good reason."

"Because I don't love you."

My usual reaction would be to take her over my knee and spank her ass for speaking lies, but I knew Cora was keeping something from me. I intended to find out what. "If you believed that, you wouldn't be here."

Cora cocked her head to the side. "What?"

"Here, in my home."

"It's your parent's home, and I love them as much as you."

I stepped away from the door and stalked toward her.

She backed up against the window, and her eyes shifted from left to right. "I have to go."

"What are you hiding, Cora?" I asked, moving close.

She placed both hands on my chest to shove me away. "What makes you think I'm hiding something?"

I grabbed her hands and pinned them against the wall above her head. "Tell me the truth."

"That is the truth. We dated, we broke up, and now you're stalking me." She paused and then mumbled. "I met someone."

Her words made my heart stop. "Who?"

She turned her face away. "You don't know him."

I gripped her chin and turned her face back to mine. "Tell me before I tear this city apart."

"You no longer control my life or emotions, EJ."

"Did you get my flowers?"

Cora twisted free of my grasp and put some distance between us. "Yes. Julia loved them."

If I didn't know her better, I'd suspect she liked it when I was riled up. I watched her pluck the photo of her mom from the dresser with shaky hands. "I remember that day."

"My eighteenth birthday." Cora smiled wistfully.

I stepped behind her. "My parents threw you a party, and I took you to the park for a picnic afterward."

"Unlike your other women, I liked you for you."

"No other woman could ever measure up to you, baby."

Cora paused for a long moment before whispering, "All I can recall is coming out of my clinic, some guy putting a gun to my head and demanding money."

It took me a few seconds to realize Cora was talking about the mugging. Her information would allow me to get video coverage of that day.

"I guess I was too slow because he hit me over the head, snatched what he could, and ran off."

"Did you see if he got in a car?"

"No." Cora put the picture back on the dresser.

"I'll have my team grab the footage."

"He needed the money more than me. I'm not worried."

"Doesn't matter. He touched you."

"We'll never be together again, EJ," Cora said with conviction.

"Cora—"

"EJ, listen. Our time together was wonderful, but we've grown up. I can't wait and wonder if you're going to just up and decide to leave me again."

My jaw clenched at her confession. "I never left you, Cora. I had obligations to my family."

"I can't compete with that, EJ. I won't." Cora kissed my cheek and walked out of the room.

* * *

All night, I replayed Cora's words in my head. I worked out until five in the morning, finally snatching an hour of sleep before the alarm went off and I headed to the office. My brothers wanted to discuss the meeting with the Vargas Cartel. Sante got word they would meet us on neutral ground at Discotech Nightclub. Our guys would be planted outside as a precaution.

"You didn't stay for dinner last night." Sante inclined in his chair.

"Not up for dinner."

"Cora looked pissed."

"I came in early to talk business, not about my love life."

Savio's eyes darkened at my bluntness. "Do we have people in place before we head to the meeting?"

"Yeah, I got the place covered," Renato answered.

"I expect you to control your temper," Savio said, standing and buttoning his jacket.

I ground my teeth. "Of all of us, I'm the least likely to lose my temper."

"Not judging by what we saw at Christmas. You were ready to kill a man right in front of your family," Renato said, rising from his chair.

"Cora told me there was only one guy who robbed her."

"Look at him, changing the subject." Renato chuckled.

"Fuck you, Renato."

"Tell Cora to do that."

Sante got between us as I charged toward Renato. "Calm down and get your fucking shit together."

A beat of tension passed before I nodded to let him know I was okay.

We headed to the elevator as Vincenzo came out of his office. "Do you need me there?"

"No. Keep things running here," Savio responded.

We took the elevator to the lobby and out to the waiting cars. The forty-minute drive passed quickly while my brothers spoke to their wives on the phone. My mind strayed to how I could get back in Cora's good graces. I needed to prove I'd changed and was no longer the immature boy who'd hurt her years ago. The family's legacy was cemented. I was a Calabresi, but I had to show her I would make her a priority.

The car stopped in front of the nightclub, and Renato gave directions to Savio and his shooters. Sante climbed out of the car after me. Savio shook hands with the guard outside the club, who opened the door for us to enter.

Darkness settled in the hallway. The guards lining both sides of the wall worked for our family and the Vargas Cartel. Savio took the lead, followed by Sante and Renato, and I brought up the rear. We entered a private room where two men were already seated. One had dark curly hair with a patch on his right eye.

"Mr. Vargas," Savio said.

"Cacho. And this is my brother, Enrique," the man said.

"Renato, Sante, Elio Jr., and you know I'm Savio." My brother introduced us, and we all took a seat.

Enrique smirked, his eyes on me as if he knew me.

"Why are you in Chicago?" Sante got right to the point.

"Business," Cacho answered.

"From what I know of your family, you stay in Mexican territory." Savio leaned forward as the bottle girl placed a bottle of bourbon in front of Enrique.

"Decided to expand."

"That doesn't work without permission," Savio said, holding Cacho's gaze.

"With all due respect, we don't need your permission." Enrique cocked his head, still staring at me.

"Business conducted in Chicago requires our permission," I explained.

"Well, well. He speaks," Enrique taunted.

I glowered at him. "What the fuck does that mean?"

Enrique pointed at me. "Aren't you the murdering lawyer?"

"We can coexist in Chicago." Cacho interrupted our stare-off.

"I like Chicago very much. The women are … exquisite." Enrique grinned.

I wanted to smack the grin off his face. "Coexisting doesn't work for us."

"Remember that our family runs deep from Chicago to Italy and South America." Savio clenched his hands.

"We agreed to this meeting as a courtesy. Chicago will be ours very soon," Enrique said with conviction.

"The Greco family and others like them tried the same thing. You may notice they're no longer around," Renato warned.

Enrique gave a humorless chuckle and spoke to his brother in Spanish. Having attended the best schools, I knew Spanish well.

"You have no clue what we're capable of. My brothers and I know your father tried the same thing, and it didn't work out for him either."

Cacho and Enrique's heads swiveled in my direction as they realized I'd understood their conversation.

"You may be surprised to know that our product is already running through the streets of Chicago," Enrique taunted.

"We know that Vargas products are already on the eastside. A courtesy on our part," Savio stated.

"Your people killed our father," Cacho revealed.

"That was years ago," Savio said.

Enrique leaned forward. "We're owed."

"Not by us," Savio replied coolly.

"We'll see," Enrique said, rising to his feet.

Cacho moved beside him as their guards closed ranks.

"We've done our research, gentlemen, and we're not

afraid of you." Enrique gave us a final smirk before the two men turned and left.

It was tempting to kill them now, but I knew that would start a war we didn't need. I bit down on my temper and let it roll off my back. People would die before all this was over, but it wouldn't be any of my loved ones. The Vargas Cartel had gone behind our backs to force us out. That wouldn't do.

"Enrique is in Cacho's ear, trying to push him forward," Sante observed. As the underboss, he could read people better than anybody.

I nodded. "I was thinking the same thing."

"Cacho's the eldest, then Izan and Enrique." Renato opened the door.

The Vargas's limos were driving off as we left the nightclub.

"Renato, I want the Eastside on lockdown," Savio instructed.

"Cut their supply." Renato grinned at the prospect of creating problems for our enemies.

"Do whatever you can to slow them down." Savio slipped into the car behind Sante as

Eunoë started the limo and pulled into traffic. "I'll work on finding out what other areas Izan is scoping out."

I gripped my phone and sent a message to Vincenzo.

Me: *Find out what Izan Vargas is working on.*

Vincenzo: *Vargas Cartel?*

Me: *Yeah, they started in the east side.*

Vincenzo: *He's a lawyer, right?*

Me: *A lawyer for the entire family. Look into Mexico and what they've been working on.*

Vincenzo: *On it.*

Me: *Thanks, and get the footage from Cora's office the night she was mugged.*

Vincenzo: *I thought she wasn't talking to you?*

Me: *She thinks she's not talking to me.*

Vincenzo: *Leave her alone if you're not serious.*

Me: *Get the information.*

Chapter 7

Cora

I refilled Anissa's glass and picked up a strawberry, dipping it in the chocolate and taking a bite. She went into detail about her date night with Mitchel, which was interrupted by an emergency at the hospital. She'd invited me over, and I wanted her to meet Rena since Mckayla and Sonya had a playdate with the kids. Like me, Devi wanted the best for Anissa, but the men she picked always came with baggage. Anissa and I met Devi in college, and we clicked right away. Her family welcomed us with open arms and nicknamed us Charlie's Angels because we did everything together. Devi's dark brown skin glowed. She looked beautiful with her tiny baby bump. Her long braids swung around her shoulders as she sat beside Anissa on the couch.

Rena grimaced. "So, he left you stranded."

I felt bad for my friend because she was in love with a man who always seemed to disappoint her at the last minute.

Anissa gulped her wine and picked up the bottle to refill her glass.

"Slow down, Anissa," I said softly.

She hiccupped and patted her chest. "I tried to ignore the signs, but maybe he's cheating."

I bit my bottom lip.

Anissa looked at me. "What do you think, Cora."

"No comment."

"You think he's cheating?" Anissa asked Devi.

"You jumped into a relationship fast," Devi remarked.

"I want what you and Wale have," Anissa murmured.

We both wanted that kind of stress-free, uncomplicated love. Devi and Wale met in college. He was a businessman who owned various companies, and Devi worked in public relations for sports teams.

"What happened with you in New York?" Devi asked me, changing the subject.

"EJ thought I'd drop everything for him, but I showed him I won't do that anymore."

"In EJ's defense, he's surrounded by egotistical men," Rena jested.

"You're married to Sante, right?" Devi asked. She knew about the family, but her job didn't leave her time to hang out as much as Anissa.

Rena picked up her fork and ate a piece of cheese and fruit from her plate. "Sante is my husband, but he acts like a child most of the time," she joked.

"EJ and I slept together," I mumbled.

Devi's mouth fell open in shock. "You slept with EJ Calabresi?"

The glee in their eyes told me I should have kept the information to myself. "Yep." I sighed and crossed my legs, leaning against the couch.

"Are you back together?" Anissa asked.

I shook my head. "No. After our night together, I left New York and returned to Chicago."

Anissa bobbed her head, scooting under the blanket on the chair. "Do you still love him?"

My head fell back in frustration. "Yes. How is that possible after everything he did to me?"

"You were young, Cora." Devi rubbed my arm comfortingly.

"EJ's human, Cora. He made a mistake," Rena added.

"I had a miscarriage," I blurted.

The room fell silent.

"You can't tell anyone, especially EJ," I whispered.

"Oh, Cora," Rena murmured.

I placed my hands in a prayer position. "Seriously, Rena, I just want to forget it happened."

"What about EJ? Doesn't he get to mourn the loss of his child? He was the father, right?" Rena cocked a brow at me.

"What are you saying?" Anissa got defensive on my behalf.

"I never cheated on EJ. I found out about the baby after we broke up. The stress brought on a miscarriage."

"I understand you wanting to protect your heart, but EJ made mistakes like we all do," Rena preached.

"I agree with Rena," Devi said.

My heart skipped a beat. What if Rena told EJ before I had the chance?

"Tell him soon," Rena urged.

"A guy asked me out at work," I confessed.

"You have all these men chasing you, and I can barely get my fiancé to go out to dinner," Anissa said dryly.

"He came into the clinic with his dog."

Rena raised an eyebrow. "Cute?"

"Very. But I turned him down. Am I crazy?"

"Yes," all three women answered at once.

I picked up a cushion and screamed into it. "He has a hold on me."

"Move on from EJ and date other people or get back with him." Rena shrugged like it was a simple solution.

I looked between my friends, searching for an answer. "What if the new guy dumps me like EJ?"

"Live life and stop with the 'what if's,' Cora," Rena advised.

"Maybe a double date with you and Sante," I suggested.

Rena chuckled like it was the stupidest idea in the world. "Sante would kill me for even suggesting a double date, especially with someone outside the family." Rena waved me off and reapplied lipstick.

"Wale is the same way. Possessive." Devi said with a smile, her hand resting on her stomach.

"Wale made sure to lock you down." I chortle, reaching for my ringing phone and glancing at a familiar number. "Oh, this is the clinic. Hold on."

"Hi, Cora. It's Julia. Sorry to bother you."

"Hey, Julia. Is everything all right at the clinic?"

"Yes. I wanted to let you know the inventory came in whenever you're ready to go through it," Julia informed me.

"Great. I'll be there tomorrow morning."

"Sounds good. Have a great evening, Cora."

"You too, Julia."

"What was that about?" Rena asked, passing some of her food to Devi.

"Inventory came in, and Julia wanted to let me know."

"Do you have to leave?" Anissa asked, popping a piece of bread into her mouth.

"Nope. Open more wine, and we can talk babies. We need to throw you a shower, Devi." I settled on the couch, placing my legs in Anissa's lap.

"I'm five months pregnant," Devi replied.

"The perfect time to throw one," Anissa said, topping up her drink.

Devi rubbed her belly. "So long as you handle all the details."

I crossed my heart and promised, pulling up the calendar on my phone.

"Great, then more power to you." Devi stood and headed for the bathroom.

"Oh, I forgot to ask. How is the robbery investigation going?" Rena asked.

I wasn't in the mood to get into that dark event. "I haven't heard from the police. EJ said he would handle finding the person."

Rena nodded. "He wants you to feel safe."

"Just promise not to sleep with him unless you're ready to commit to a relationship, or you'll end up like me. Dating a man who drives you to consider getting a cat and living alone." Anissa sighed dramatically.

Rena and I giggled, and Anissa hurled a pillow at us.

* * *

I tended to work at odd hours and asked some of my staff to come in early to do an inventory and clean the entire place before it opened. The weekend hours weren't long like the weekdays, so opening at noon and closing at five gave us plenty of time to ensure the work was correctly logged without rushing through clients.

"Hair down and casual clothes. You must've had a great night," Julia teased, passing me one of the shampoo bottles we ordered for the clinic.

I perched on the step stool and placed it on the top shelf. "I spent some time with the girls last night."

"Can't think of the last time you hung out for fun."

"They told me I work too much."

Julia passed me another bottle. "Maybe you should take that guy up on his offer of a date."

"What guy?"

"The one with the bulldog. Enrique."

My cheeks flushed. "Probably has a wife or girlfriend."

"You won't know if you don't call him."

"I didn't get his number."

"He left his information," Julia said, looking him up in our system.

A commotion from the front entrance drew my attention. I climbed down from the step and headed to the front office to find Colson, my staff member, yelling at someone at the front door. A tall gentleman stood there holding a briefcase.

"Is there something I can help you with?" I asked, annoyed that he'd ignored the 'closed' sign on the door.

He scowled. "You can tell your assistant to let me in so I can talk to you."

"We're closed." Colson placed his arm across the door to prevent him from entering.

The man looked at Colson with disdain. "I'm not here with a sick pet."

"Okay, so what do you want, Mr ...?"

The man reached into his pocket, pulled out an envelope, and handed it to me. "My name is irrelevant. My client would like to buy your building."

I glared at the envelope. "I've already made it clear I won't sell."

The man's expression revealed nothing. "My client is offering you a good price. You should take it. This place doesn't look like it'll be around for much longer."

"Izan Cumin," I repeated the name on the business card I'd tossed a few days ago.

He pushed his hand into his pocket and sighed. "Think about the amount of money."

I held onto my temper. "Drug money." I tossed the envelope back at him. "I am not for sale."

"That's too bad. I heard about the accident a few weeks ago," he said.

His remark took me aback. "How do you know about that?"

"News travels fast."

"Leave, or I'll call the police!" I shouted, slamming the door in his face.

"What happened to the security you told me about?" Colson demanded.

I looked out the window and saw one of the soldiers EJ had hired motioning for our unwelcome visitor to leave.

"He's taking care of him now." I glanced at my watch and directed Colson to start the morning chores before opening.

Returning to my office, I picked up the phone and called EJ.

"Cora?" he answered on the first ring.

"EJ, any news on the robbery?"

"No. Vincenzo is getting the footage for me. Why?"

"Might be nothing." I placed my hand on my hip.

"Tell me, Cora."

"A guy just came to my clinic with an envelope full of money."

"Where are the soldiers I put on your block?"

"Outside with him. Well, I think they're still with him."

"Did he touch you?"

"No. Sorry for calling. I can handle it myself."

"No, you won't. I'll handle anyone who tries to hurt you."

I smiled at his vehemence. "Thanks. Sorry to bother you at work."

"Work is work. I'm texting the boys to get updates now."

"Then I'll get off the phone."

"I like listening to you talk," he growled.

I chuckled. "EJ, you're an asshole. How many times have you told me I talk too much?"

His laugh rumbled down the line. "It's true, especially when we were watching a movie.

"It's not my fault I predicted the Halloween movies."

"Have dinner with me, Cora," he said suddenly.

His request took me off-guard. "EJ, we discussed this already."

"*You* discussed it. I disagreed, and I haven't changed my mind."

"One-sided relationships don't work."

"Baby, our relationship has never been one-sided. We have too much history."

"More than you know," I said under my breath, my secret weighing heavily on me.

"Huh?"

"Uh, nothing."

"Please have dinner with me, Cora. We can finally talk."

It was satisfying to hear him beg. "Even if I still don't want to be with you afterward?"

"Damn, you're stubborn."

A wry smile twisted my mouth. "I told you I plan to date other people, and you want to stop it. But what about you and other women?"

"The only woman for me is you."

"Empty flattery, EJ."

"Dinner. I'll pick you up at nine." EJ tries to have the last word.

"There's the bossy EJ I know."

"You know it."

I end the call and sit behind my desk. Pushing thoughts of EJ aside, I busy myself with work. A few hours later, I'm interrupted by a knock at the door.

"Come in!"

Astonished by my visitor, I stood and walked around my desk to meet him halfway. "Enrique."

"I wanted to bring Princess in so you can see she's doing better." He lifted her, and I stroked her head.

Our eyes met. "Nice to see you both, but you didn't have to come here."

Enrique stretched his hand out to take my palm. "I do have an alternative motive."

I raised an eyebrow in question.

"Would you do me the honor of having dinner with me as a thank you?"

"I'm sorry, I have plans."

A smile quickly replaced his frown. "It seems I have competition."

I laughed. Having a client hit on me was new. I usually met guys at clubs or out drinking with the girls.

"No competition. I said I'd have dinner with my ex tonight."

He smiled. "Enjoy your dinner. Maybe we can do something tomorrow?"

I pulled my hand from his. "You're a client."

Enrique closed the space between us. "In that case, you're fired. I'll find another vet."

I chuckled and shook my head. "Really?"

"Princess says you have to agree to dinner," Enrique cajoled.

As if on cue, she flashed me her puppy dog eyes. I raised my index finger. "One dinner."

"Fantastic. I'll call you." He grinned and winked at me.

I gave him a curious look. "You don't have my number."

"I got it last time from your staff."

"Oh."

Enrique seemed determined. He reminded me of EJ. I liked a man who knew what he wanted and went after it.

"I look forward to seeing you outside these walls, Cora."

I smiled. "Me too."

He raised my hand to his mouth and kissed my knuckles. "Have a good day."

"You too, Enrique."

Once Enrique left, I finished the rest of the day in a

daze. I'd agreed to back-to-back dates with two strong-willed men who both wanted me.

* * *

Later that night, I slipped my gold bracelet onto my wrist and applied my favorite red lipstick. I turned in the bathroom mirror and fluffed my hair one more time. I checked the clock as the doorbell rang. EJ was five minutes early. I slipped my feet into my black heels and slid into my jacket. Grabbing my purse and phone, I walked down the hall of my apartment to answer the door.

"Hey, Cora," EJ greeted me. "These are for you." He handed me a boutique of red roses.

I dipped my head to inhale their delicate aroma. "Thank you. Let me put them in water."

I turned and left him on the doorstep while I found a vase in the kitchen, filled it with water, and placed the roses inside.

"Where are we going for dinner?" I asked as I rejoined him.

"Prosecco."

"Sounds like a normal date for once."

"Give me credit for trying, Cora."

"For doing what you're supposed to do, EJ?"

He caught my elbow, and I looked down at his hand. A shock wave of sensation hit me like it always did when he touched me. I should cut him out of my life the way he did to me all those years ago, but deep down, I knew it wouldn't work. We were too deeply connected.

"Are you going to allow me to make things right, or have I lost you already?" he asked gruffly.

"I'll never turn my back on you, EJ. But I need to protect my heart."

He drew me close, stroking the back of my neck. "The last thing I ever wanted to do was break your heart, but I'm not perfect and never proclaimed to be."

A million butterflies took flight in my stomach at the intensity in his eyes. "At least you're being honest."

"So answer my question."

"Can we get through dinner first?"

Leaning forward, he kissed me on the forehead. "You look beautiful."

I closed my eyes briefly at the tender gesture. "Thank you. You look handsome."

EJ stepped back while I locked the door. Taking my hand, he led me to the elevator. I pushed the button, and our eyes met as we waited.

Outside, EJ helped me into the Bentley before climbing into the driver's seat.

"Where's your guard?"

"Around, but I wanted to have alone time with you." EJ planted a hand on my thigh as he drove through the streets toward Prosecco.

Chapter 8

Elio Jr

Cora scanned the restaurant. Most people came out with their significant other on Saturday nights. Instead of shutting the place down, I booked a private table, ensuring it was still in an area where she would feel comfortable. Cora was the only woman I took on dates and showered with gifts. Other women wished they were in her position. Something about that made me feel small because I no longer had her trust.

"If you don't mind, I had them present the menu with all your favorites."

Our waitress set the bottle of Syrah and Sangiovese on the table. I picked it up and poured a small amount into our glasses.

"*Cozze e Vongole* and *Tartufata*," Cora said.

"Plus, dessert afterward at your favorite ice cream shop."

"I'm being spoiled, and it's not my birthday." Her brows drew together, and she pressed her lips into a cute pout.

"It's my way of starting over with you."

Cora extended her hand. "Hello, I'm Cora."

I smile. "I'm EJ."

"Nice to meet you, EJ. Do you come here often?"

Knowing we were in a crowded restaurant did nothing to subdue my hard-on. Cora's pouty lips formed a heart shape, begging to be kissed.

"You are dangerous, Cora." I took a swing of my wine.

"How so?"

"Stunning. Beautiful. I'll worship you until the day I die."

She gasped at my words. "I put you on a pedestal EJ."

"What does that mean?"

"You said you'd worship me, and I realized I'd do the same with you. I put more pressure on you than I should have."

I reached across the table and covered her hand with mine. "Hey, never question my love for you."

"I know you love me. We were both kids back then, and I put pressure on you that you had no hope of living up to at twenty. You were discovering who you were and what you wanted out of life."

"If I'd married you, do you think we'd still be together?"

Cora dropped her eyes, giving me her answer. "Honestly, I think I would have wanted a divorce. Being a wife in your world would probably make me angry and resentful."

I agreed with her, but her words still stung. My parent's marriage of over thirty-five years wasn't all roses and rainbows. Marriage took time, and if you truly loved that person, it was worth all the drama.

Our meals were brought to the table, and Cora picked

up her fork, taking the first bite. "Oh, my god. So good." She moaned and took another bite.

"Keep moaning like that, Cora," I growled. "I'm happy you're enjoying it, but save room for dessert."

She saluted me, and I laughed at her silliness. I'd missed that.

"How is business at Calabresi Inc?"

"Business is fine. A lot of contracts have come across my desk."

"Being a billionaire, do you even think about it all the time?"

"No, but you'll know what it's like as soon as we're married."

Cora laughed. "There you go on the first date."

"Stating my intentions now." I lifted her hand and kissed her knuckles.

She hesitated and squeezed my hand. "Can I tell you something, and you not get mad?"

"Go ahead, Cora."

"I have a date tomorrow."

"Cancel it."

"Elio, you said you wouldn't get mad."

"I'm not mad, but you're not going on a date unless I take you out."

"Elio."

Cora always called me by my full name when she was pissed. I liked how her little nose scrunched up when she was angry.

"Cora, I want you to be happy, and I know I'm the person who can give you that. I can't imagine the man you're going on a date with tomorrow night making you happy."

Cora's mouth opened in shock, but before she could

respond, the server arrived.

"Do you need anything else?" she questioned.

"We're fine, thanks," I replied with a smile.

"It's hard to believe you won't let me be happy," Cora said as the server retreated.

"You made me fall in love with you."

Throwing her head back, Cora cackled and waved her hand in the air. "EJ, you make no sense. How is it my fault you fell in love with me?"

I shrugged. "Great pussy."

"Is that all?"

"No. I love your mind and how you challenge me. I love how close you are to your mother. I know how close you two are. It's the same for my mother and me."

"My mind, huh? You always did copy my homework," she teased.

She was right. But she got her revenge when we played board games.

"You can't deny I'm better with you."

Happiness spread over her face. We continued talking about our relationship hits and misses for the rest of dinner. After paying, I drove to Cora's favorite ice cream shop before returning to her place.

"Are you coming up?" Cora asked as I parked outside.

"I get an invite upstairs? Does that mean I did good so far?"

"So far?" She waited for me to open her door.

I grabbed the leftover ice cream and slid her hand into mine. Closing the door behind us, I escorted her up to her apartment.

Cora opened the door, and we went inside. She took the ice cream from my hand and put it in the freezer. I removed my coat and placed it over the back of the sofa, walking around her to look at the pictures on her walls.

"Do you want coffee or more wine?" Cora asked.

I put the picture of her when she was ten back on the mantel. "Water is fine."

"Coming right up."

I went to sit and saw her computer open on the sofa. As I picked it up, a new message popped up on the screen from Anissa.

"*Did you tell him about the baby?*"

I stared at the computer in shock. Cora was pregnant? Why the hell hadn't she told me? I remembered we hadn't used protection in New York.

"Here's the water, and I made you a cup of coffee." Cora passed me the bottle of water.

I put it on the table and stared at her stomach.

Cora shifted uneasily. "What's wrong?"

"Are you pregnant?" I turned the computer to face her.

"You read my messages!" Cora accused.

"Tell me the truth. Are you pregnant?"

"No."

"Don't lie to me, Cora."

"There's something I never told you."

I grit my teeth to control my temper. "I'm listening." If she were about to tell me about another guy, I wouldn't be responsible for my actions.

Cora dropped her eyes and murmured. "I had a miscarriage."

I shook my head in confusion. "Wait, you just said you weren't pregnant."

"I was."

I paced back and forth. "Cora, start making sense because you're pissing me off."

"I found out I was pregnant right after you broke up with me, and the stress caused me to have a miscarriage." Cora wiped a tear from her cheek.

Memories flooded my mind. How Cora had distanced herself during those first few weeks after we broke up. I'd asked Marilyn where Cora was a few days afterward, and she'd told me that Cora was spending some time traveling.

"Miscarriage," I whispered.

"I wanted to tell you, Elio." Cora reached for my hand.

I stepped back, not ready for her to touch me. "I need a minute, Cora." I grabbed my coat and keys.

"Elio! Where are you going?" Cora followed me to the door.

"Lock up. I'll call you later."

"Elio, please talk to me." Cora tugged at my jacket.

I paused with my hand on the door handle. "Cora, let me go."

"No."

"I promise to call you later. I need to process everything."

She released me, and I left without looking back. I hopped in my car, pulled into traffic, and sped toward the bar.

Had Cora deliberately kept her miscarriage from me?

Do I really know her?

We'd never kept secrets. What else was she keeping from me? I slammed my hand on the steering wheel, running a red light as I swerved to avoid a car. Finally, I found a bar and ambled in to drink all thoughts from my brain.

"Neat bourbon," I told the bartender.

"Tab?" he asked.

I nodded.

The clock on the wall said midnight. I tossed the bourbon back and motioned for another, peering around the room. A hand fell on my shoulder as I reached into my pocket to grab my phone. I looked up to see Renato.

"How did you know I was here?"

"Cora called me. Said you were upset."

Renato stood at the bar, facing the crowd. Freddie appeared, and I realized he'd been trailing me all night. He must have called Renato.

"You think that's the answer?" Renato pointed at the drink in my hand.

I gulped it down and asked for another. "Something stronger."

"How many has he had?" Renato asked the bartender, who avoided eye contact with him.

"I'm not a kid, Renato." I shrugged his hand off my shoulder.

Renato leaned on the bar top. "You need to sleep it off."

"No, what I need is my child!" I barked.

"Walk with me." Renato extended his arm around my shoulder.

I followed him outside and breathed in the night air. Cora's words were like a knife to my heart. "She was pregnant, Renato."

Renato angled me in the direction of the car. "I heard."

I stopped, and my head swiveled toward him. "You knew?"

He sighed. "She told me when she called."

"I wonder if Madre knew."

"No way."

"How can you be so sure? She loves Cora like a daughter."

Renato held out his hand. "Give me your keys."

"I'm fine."

"EJ, hand them over."

I dropped the keys into his hand, and he passed them to Freddie.

"She told me she has a date tomorrow." I chuckled and climbed into the passenger seat of Renato's car.

"With who?" he asked, settling into the driver's seat.

"I don't know. Cora's trying to hurt me."

"Once you sleep it off, you'll figure shit out." Renato patted me on the back.

Renato started the car and turned on his signal light. He paused when a vehicle pulled alongside us with blacked-out windows.

"You carrying?" Renato asked urgently.

"Always."

Before Renato and I could react, the window lowered, and a lit bottle mocktail was launched into the street in front of us.

Renato swerved to avoid it. "Motherfuckers!"

He sped up to chase the vehicle. I rolled my window down and fired at the rear tire.

"Call Savio!" Renato barked.

I emptied my clip, hit the Bluetooth in his car, and waited for the dial tone to pick up.

"Renato, it's midnight," Mckayla answered groggily.

"Mckayla, I need to talk to Savio." I heard rustling in the background as Mckayla tried to wake up Savio.

"What?" Savio grumbled at the end of the line.

"We ran out of milk."

"Spoiled?"

"Deadly."

"Go directly to the store, and I'll order a caseload."

I ended the call. Renato turned off the main street to avoid being ambushed and headed to the office. I kept an eye out for any other suspicious vehicles. Fifteen minutes later, he stopped in front of the building. We hopped out, and Freddie was already there with his automatic rifle. Security opened the door, and we headed to the elevator, pushing the button for the basement.

I texted Savio to get security, asking him to check on Cora in case I'd been followed to her house. "You get the license plate number?" I asked Renato.

"No, but we know it was Vargas's people." His eyes were fixed on the basement door. He unlocked it, and we went inside. I took a seat as the door opened, and Savio and Sante entered, escorted by Jason.

"What happened?" Savio was dressed in casual black slacks and a white shirt, his hair ruffled.

"I picked EJ up from the bar, and as we were leaving, someone pulled up alongside and set off a bomb mocktail."

"Anyone hurt?" Sante asked.

"No," I replied.

Sante looked at Renato. "Who do you think it was?"

"Vargas. The only enemy we have."

"Why were you at the bar alone?" Savio wondered.

"I didn't know I had to account for my whereabouts," I snapped.

Savio glared at me.

"He had a date with Cora." Renato tried to ease the tension.

"You put her in danger," Savio snarled, his eyes narrowed.

I grit my teeth. "You know me better than that. Cora's safe with me."

"Not when bombs are being thrown around," Savio chastised.

"Fuck you, Savio!" I jumped out of my seat, and Renato pushed me back down.

Savio acted like he'd never had to endure bullshit to get Mckayla. I couldn't think straight between Cora's confession and the Vargas attack.

My eyes seared toward Savio and Sante. "Did you know about Cora's miscarriage?"

Sante's eyebrows rose. "Cora was pregnant?"

Hearing it out loud from my brother hit me even harder. Cora was pregnant. *Pregnant* and had miscarried because of me. I hadn't been there to help her handle the loss. All the time we'd missed together could have been avoided if we'd had a conversation and reconnected. Work with the cartel had consumed me. When I first became a lawyer, work was nonstop. I was always traveling, living out of a suitcase at one hotel after another.

"She was," I said flatly.

Savio sighed. "I'm sorry about Cora. Can you handle what's coming?"

My thumb hovered over Cora's name on my phone. "When have you ever questioned me on handling Cartel business?"

"EJ, we've all gone through our share of problems, but

you've had a longer connection with Cora, and she's like a sister to the rest of us."

"I can handle it, Savio."

"He's good, Savio. The problem is Vargas." Renato backed me up.

Savio loosened up. "You're right. Did you see the drivers?"

"No." Renato and I answered in unison.

"Send a counter message," Savio instructed.

"I want in," I said.

Sante shook his head. "Renato can handle it alone. As the lawyer and public figure, you shouldn't be anywhere near whatever happens."

"I know what I'm doing, Sante."

"Sante's right, EJ," Savio argued.

Savio was dealing me out, but I needed to put a mark on the people who'd tried to kill us tonight. Renato discussed how he'd get to Vargas, and I agreed to wait to make a move until we had another meeting with Enrique.

After talking with my brothers, I had Renato drop me off at home, showered, and passed out in bed.

Chapter 9

Cora

A month passed, and I still felt awful about how EJ had found out about the baby. He'd ignored all my calls that night and the following week. Adelina had invited me to a family dinner, but he didn't show. I knew this news would create a divide between his family and me. My mother told me everybody was fine, but I'd had a conversation with Adelina, and she was upset.

"EJ told me what happened," Adelina said.

Bile filled my throat. If Adelina despised me, I knew the entire family would never speak to me again. "Do you hate me?"

Adelina rested a hand on my arm. "No, but I wish I'd known."

Tears dripped down my cheeks. "He hates me."

"Elio loves you, Cora." Adelina cupped my cheek.

"Have you talked to him?"You

"Work has kept him busy. Give him time. Cora. you two will figure it out," Adelina said.

"I told him I have a date with someone else."

"You two are like trains, never connecting at the same time."

"I feel terrible that he's hurt."

"Do you love him? What to be with him?"

"I think the baby situation and where we are in life has complicated us being together."

"If I know anything, EJ will come for you. Give him space. But be sure you know what you want out of life."

"Thank you, Adelina."

"But don't wait too long. The thought of more grand-children makes me happy."

Since that day, I'd poured all my time into work and hanging with my friends. Enrique had texted again to rearrange our date after I'd canceled. Adelina's comments about being sure what I wanted had made me think hard about dating someone else.

"Hey, Cora." Mitchel opened the door. I waved at him. He opened the door wider I saw their dog behind him.

"Cora! Glad you're here." Anissa held out a cup of coffee for me. I took it and followed her to the living room.

"Babe, I'm leaving for work," Mitchel told Anissa.

She stood to kiss him on the lips. "Call me later when you go on break."

"I took today off. What are we doing?"

Anissa said, picking up her cell phone and sending a text. "Devi's baby shower. I was thinking we could go look at locations."

"We should go shopping."

"We can." She eyed me. "You look refreshed."

"Finally got some sleep last night."

Anissa placed her phone away. "Have you talked to EJ since that night?"

"No."

"You know what you need to do."

"What?"

"Go to his house and force him to talk to you."

"EJ's not like that."

"Mitchel and I had an argument and stopped talking for two days before I forced him to listen to me."

I removed my jacket and sipped on my drink. "I talked to his mother."

"How did that go?"

"She understood. She advised me to figure out if I want to be with EJ or move on with my life."

Anissa grabbed her car keys and purse. "When the mother-in-law wants you two to be together, you have to wonder what's important."

"What if we start over, and he breaks up with me again?"

"Then you move on and find another man to keep you warm at night. Like that Enrique guy." Anissa shimmed her shoulders, and I laughed.

She locked the door behind us, and we headed to my car. I watched Anissa type in the address of the first location, and we took off, taking the freeway.

"Enrique texted me again."

"When?"

"A few days ago about going on a date."

"Are you going?"

"Would I be a terrible person if I went out with another guy?"

Anissa counted on her hand, "In your twenties, unmarried, no kids, a great job. Date whoever you want."

I leaned my forehead on the steering wheel as I stopped in traffic. "One date won't hurt," I muttered.

Anissa advised, "Make sure it's what you want to do and not out of obligation."

I groaned and hit the gas pedal, moving forward. Was I ready to have a future without Elio Jr.?

We reached downtown Chicago, and I parked at the Beachy Banquet Hall. We climbed out of the car, and Anissa pushed the buzzer out front. Security opened the door.

"Hi, we wanted to check out the space for an event," Anissa said.

"Go to the front desk, and they'll help you," he replied.

The half-hour walk-through of the place went well, and then we met up with Devi and Rena for lunch.

"I like that place. You should put a deposit down." Anissa slipped her seatbelt on.

I started the car. "We can double-check with Devi. I'm fine to have it there."

"Great. Oh, I forgot to tell you; Mitchel and I are fine now."

"Did he tell you why he's working long hours?"

"No, but I trust him."

Anissa's situation with Mitchel made me think of EJ and me and how easily things unraveled if you didn't communicate.

* * *

Anissa had the server send peach lemonades to our table, and we headed to our booth to eat. Rena was already seated, and I hugged her, then Sonya.

"Glad you two could get away to hang out." I laid my jacket on my lap.

"Sonya's been stuck on mommy duty forever," Rena jested.

"Renato wants a fleet of kids. I'm trying to balance it all," Sonya said.

The server appeared with our drinks. I took a gulp and flipped open the menu.

"Girls, I'm here." Devi waved at us, and Anissa moved over to give her room to sit down.

"We ordered you a peach lemonade," Anissa said, picking up the menu as the server waited for our order.

"I'm starving." Rena rubbed her stomach.

Sonya gave her order to the server and turned to me. "How is work, Cora?"

"Busy. I need to go by there and check on things."

"EJ found out anything about finding the person who robbed you?"

"No, we haven't talked in a few weeks."

"Because of the baby thing?" Sonya asked.

The table went quiet.

I shifted awkwardly in my seat and cleared my throat. "Yeah, he found out in the worst way. Plus, he's busy." I'd promised myself I'd give EJ space and not hound him. I'd had time to grieve, and he needed the same.

"Did he tell you about the car chase?" Rena asked.

"Car chase?"

"After he left your place that night, he ended up at a bar. Renato showed up to take him home, and someone threw a mocktail bomb in the middle of the street."

My stomach dropped. "I need to call him."

Rena frowned. "First, you were robbed, and now this. Something doesn't add up."

I smiled at the server. "Can I get the sushi platter, please?"

"Be right back." She grabbed our menus and left the table.

Rena explained that the footage they'd captured showed a side profile of the person who'd robbed me. "I took a screenshot of him," she said, looking pleased with herself.

"Do you recognize him?" Devi asked.

I stared at the photo of the tall figure. "No clue."

"Be extra careful when you leave work." Devi took a sip of her water.

"One thing EJ does is make sure I'm safe."

"Which means you don't need to go on this date with the other guy."

"What guy?" Rena perked up.

"He came into the clinic with his dog. He's mysterious and sexy." Anissa grinned.

"Did you get his number?" Sonya asked.

"He texted me, but I don't know if I want to go out with him," I replied.

"Because of EJ?" Sonya enquired.

The server arrived at the table to deliver our food, and the conversation changed to Devi's baby shower we were throwing for her in a few weeks. After lunch, I dropped Anissa back home and went to the clinic to check over some paperwork and emails. As I locked the car door and turned, I bumped into a hard body.

"Careful," a sexy voice said, steadying me with his hands on my arms.

I smiled up at Enrique. "What are you doing here? Is Princess sick again?"

"No. I wanted to check up on you."

"That's sweet, but I'm fine." I stepped out of his grip and headed to the clinic's front door.

"Let me get the door for you."

"Thanks."

"Have you given any thought to our dinner?"

"Hey, boss lady," Julia called out from reception.

"Hi, Julia. Any calls? You remember Enrique."

"Yes. How are you, Enrique?"

"I'd be better if this beautiful woman took me up on my dinner offer." Enrique pointed at me.

I laughed. "He's a charmer, but I can't."

"Are you involved with somebody?" A flash of anger appeared on his face for a split second.

"You don't have any calls, but there's a surprise in your office," Julia said, saving me from answering.

"A surprise?"

"My competition, possibly," Enrique waggled his eyebrows, and Julia giggled.

His appearance out of the blue made me uncomfortable, but he was new in town and probably didn't have many friends. "You didn't say if Princess was sick or not?"

Enrique lagged behind me as I walked to my office. I opened the door and came to an abrupt halt.

"What the fuck is this?"

EJ was sitting at my desk, and my entire office was filled with flowers.

"EJ?" My eyes widened, and I took a step back.

His face distorted in rage, and he growled, "Have you lost your goddamn mind?"

"What?" A stab of guilt tightened my stomach.

EJ moved around the desk. "Get the fuck away from her."

I stepped in front of Enrique, holding up my hand to block him. "EJ, what's wrong with you?"

EJ reached behind him, pulling his gun. "Cora, leave the room."

My mouth dropped open in shock. "This is my place of business."

"*Hermosa*, I take it this is your ex?" Enrique asked smoothly.

That pissed EJ off even more because he lifted the gun and pointed it at his head. EJ's eyes stayed on Enrique as he asked, "How do you know him, Cora?"

"Who?"

EJ cocked the gun. "Enrique Vargas."

"Enrique Vargas?" I frowned.

"I guess that means our date is postponed," Enrique taunted him.

I turned to face him. "Did you know who I was?"

Enrique smirked but kept his eyes trained on EJ. "Call me when you're ready to be with a real man."

He extended a hand to cup my chin. EJ yanked me back by my elbow and lunged at Enrique.

"Elio!" I screamed, stumbling backward.

EJ lifted his gun to Enrique's face.

"Stop it!" I shouted.

"Cora, what's going on in here?" Colson stood at the door.

I reached for Elio's arm. "Colson, help me pull them apart."

Before Enrique could hit EJ, another staff member stepped in and helped Colson break them up.

"Get off me!" EJ yelled at Colson.

"Enrique, go, please," I begged.

He wiped the blood from his lip and hiked his

brow. "We'll meet again," Enrique tilted his chin in a challenge before he left my office.

I reached for EJ, but he stepped back as if I'd hurt him.

"Are you all right, Cora?" Colson asked.

"I'm fine, Colson, thank you."

"You're sleeping with him?" EJ demanded.

I looked at him in confusion. "What?"

EJ's face was a mask of anger. "Did you sleep with our enemy?"

Angry heat hit my cheeks. "Elio, calm down."

"Answer me, Cora," EJ snapped, darkness clouding his features. He looked like a stranger.

"I haven't heard from you in a month, and you come here demanding to know about my personal life?" I knew it wasn't wise to deflect his question, but I was tired of being kept in the dark until he was ready to notice me again.

He crowded me, grabbing my chin and forcing me to look at him. The hurt in his eyes told me he thought I'd betrayed him.

"I didn't sleep with him," I whispered.

"I know. I'm sorry." EJ caressed my cheek and crushed his lips to mine. I should be pushing him away, but instead, my arms wound around his neck, and I moaned as he cupped my ass.

We were both breathless when he pulled back.

"I'm sorry about not telling you," I said, lowering my walls.

He shook his head. "Not here."

"EJ, we have to talk."

"Get your things."

"For what?"

"You're coming with me."

"Where?"

"Get your stuff, Cora."

"No." I stepped around him and folded my arms over my chest.

"Either you come with me now, or I shut this place down."

We glared at each other. I'd missed him during the last month, and I needed answers about Enrique.

"Fine, I'll go with you, but don't think you're off the hook for fighting in my place of business."

EJ took me by the hand, and we walked down the hall to let my staff know I was leaving.

"Julia, make sure you lock up my office," I told my assistant.

Julia looked concerned. "Is everything all right?"

"Everything's fine. You can close early today."

"We need to go." EJ tugged on my hand.

I followed him outside to his town car, where Freddie was waiting. EJ helped me inside. "Where are we going?"

"My place." He dropped my hand and pulled out his phone.

"Who are you texting?"

EJ ignored my question and lifted his phone to his ear. "How do you know Enrique?"

I scooted up to talk to Freddie in the driver's seat. "Freddie, drop me off at my place."

Freddie glanced at EJ in the rearview mirror.

"To my house," EJ instructed.

I glowered. "I don't take orders from you."

"Savio, we have a problem." EJ ignored me as he spoke on the phone.

"God, you're impossible!" I huffed. I moved to the corner of the car and faced the window.

I listened to EJ and Savio go back and forth about what happened as we headed to his home. I'd started my day wondering when I'd get to see EJ after almost a month, only to witness him in a fight with Enrique.

Fifteen minutes later, we arrived at his home. I shoved the car door open without waiting for Freddie and stomped toward the front door.

"I'll call you back." EJ finished his call and unlocked the front door. "Wait for me inside," he instructed.

"You have five minutes, or I'm leaving."

He ignored my comment as another car pulled into the driveway. My phone was snatched from my hand as I pulled it from my pocket to call Anissa to pick me up.

"Give me my phone," I demand, trying to hold onto my temper.

"Who are you calling?"

"Does it matter?"

EJ frowned as he scrolled through my phone before shoving it into his pocket.

"Tell me what's going on, EJ, or I will walk out of here."

"Enrique Vargas is the head of the Vargas Cartel."

A host of thoughts crowded my mind. EJ keeping me out of the loop at this point would only prove his lack of trust in me. "And?"

"Did you hear what I just said?"

I was no stranger to cartel life. I'd grown up around the Calabresis'. "Yeah, he's a mobster."

"A very dangerous cartel leader. You could get hurt."

"I understand cartel life very well. You chose it over me," I snapped.

EJ swiftly lifted me and carried me to the couch as I turned to walk away. "He's trying to take over Chicago. He knows damn well who you are."

"He came into my clinic because his dog was sick."

"Cora, you're not naive."

His comment sparked my annoyance. "Move, EJ."

"Is he the one who asked you on a date?"

"I haven't seen you in a month, and that's your question?"

"You can't see him again."

"He showed up out of the blue today."

Sante appeared in the doorway. "EJ, we need to talk."

EJ kissed me on the forehead. "I need to go take care of something."

"What makes you think I'll be here when you get back?"

"There's food in the kitchen. I'll be back." He leaned in and kissed me softly.

I should've pushed him away, but longing still burned within me to make things right between us, even if we only ended up as friends.

Chapter 10

Elio Jr

Sante and Renato spent an hour trying to calm me down. All I wanted to do was kill Enrique with my bare hands. The motherfucker thought he could touch what belonged to me, and I wouldn't find out. Cora being in his presence pushed my buttons. I knew he'd manipulated her in some way. She'd help anybody if they asked. No doubt he'd gone to her with a sob story.

My mother had told me she was pissed when I'd avoided the family dinners, and they'd discussed my finding out about Cora's miscarriage. It took a few weeks for me to come to grips with our loss. I understood now how certain decisions impacted others, and I had regrets.

Renato and I finally got the license plate of the man who assaulted and robbed Cora. Renato also took care of Vargas's product on the east side by calling in a favor with a few of our lower-level dealers.

"Where is he?" I entered the warehouse after leaving Cora at my place.

"Waiting for you," Renato responded and slid the door open.

I looked at the two men tied up with duct tape and blindfolds covering their eyes. "Did you get people over to Cora's office?"

"Yeah, her staff said no one came in after she left."

"I need to talk to her about closing the place down or relocating."

"She won't like that," Renato said, knowing how stubborn she could be.

"Too bad." I stalked over and ripped the masks off both men, waiting for their eyes to adjust to the light. "I'll make your deaths quick if you're truthful."

They nodded, and I ripped the tape off their mouths. "Where is Enrique Vargas?"

"Fuck!" one of the men shouted in pain.

I took the gun out of Renato's hand and cocked it. "You have five seconds."

"We didn't mean to hurt her," The other man spoke first.

"Why did you rob her?"

"He told us it was a simple job, but she wouldn't let the purse go," the guy with a busted lip blurted.

"And the car chase?"

He lowered his head. "He paid us to scare you."

"What else did he plan?"

"We don't know," he said in a rush. "Last time we heard from him, he told us to follow you for a little while."

"Why were you following Cora before you robbed her place?"

They went silent.

"Answer me!" I barked.

The ringleader nodded. "Look, we didn't know it was your girl."

I smirked. "How is your mother on 23rd and Spring Street, Anthony."

His nostrils flared. "Leave my family out of this."

"You started this. Now I have to retaliate in kind." It was time to end them once and for all.

"Our families have nothing to do with Vargas," Anthony pleaded.

"Nothing is fair in this world. Vargas should have told you about us."

Renato flipped his phone and showed them a picture of Anthony's son's school. Enrique had paid two idiots who thought I'd let their attempts to harm my family slide. Seeing Cora in a hospital bed because of their actions pissed me off.

"We can help you. I know where Vargas is staying," Anthony offered desperately.

"Where?" I already knew his location, but it wouldn't hurt to have Anthony confirm it.

"Promise you won't touch my son or mother."

"Wrong answer." I turned the gun on his partner and shot him between the eyes.

Blood splattered all over Anthony's face. "What the fuck?" he shrieked. "Please, he's just a kid. I can help you."

"You touched my girl thinking we wouldn't catch you."

"Enrique's not done!" Anthony confessed, his eyes begging me to believe him.

Some people believed I didn't have a heart, but I would never harm a child. They were innocent of their father's sins. On the other hand, making an example of Anthony would draw out Enrique, so I could kill him before he made another move.

"I have way more reach than Enrique Vargas. You chose the wrong side, Anthony."

I shot him in the head and handed the gun to Renato. Walking up to his dead body, I kicked him in the chest.

The ringing of Renato's phone brought me out of my trance.

"He did what?" Renato demanded, his brows pinched with anger.

"Clean up this mess," I commanded our soldiers.

Renato ended the call. "We need to go."

"Who was that?"

"Pops."

"He's not getting involved. He can't stop what's happening here."

"I agree, but we need to go see him." Renato and I left the warehouse and drove to our parents' house.

"You need to check in on Cora," Renato said.

My eyes were glued to Cora's text message thread I'd ignored for a month. Would we ever get back on the same page? Had I pushed her away for good? Whatever happened with us, I wouldn't let her endanger herself with Enrique.

Me: *We need to talk.*

I hit "send" as Renato shifted the car into the park outside our parents'. I stepped out of the car and jogged up the steps, leaving Renato to follow me. Shoving my phone in my pocket, I strolled down the hall to my father's office, opening the door to find him on the phone.

"Enrique Vargas is a dead man," I snapped.

Father ended his call and gave me a stern look. "Sit down."

Renato glanced at me as he entered the office and shut the door.

"Enrique Vargas made contact with Cora. He set up the robbery," I told my father.

He nodded. "I know. It will be handled."

I narrowed my eyes at him, gripping the back of the chair. "Handled, how?"

"Vincenzo told me what you discovered."

"How are you handling Vargas?" I challenged.

"A truce needs to be made."

My lip twitched at the suggestion. Why the hell would he think I'd sit down with the man who'd tried to hurt my girl?

"I have to disagree, Pops." Renato backed me up, his tone measured.

My father remained calm, as usual. "Sit down, EJ."

I sank into the chair opposite his desk. "You know what the Vargas Cartel is capable of and want me to let it go?"

"We've been hit too many times. We need to make amends for the sake of appearances." My father's suggestions only pissed me off more. "Fuck appearances!"

He slammed his hand on the desk. "You will not disrespect me in my home!"

I didn't recognize this man. He didn't seem like the person I'd known all my life. "What are they paying you?"

"EJ," Renato warned.

I shook my head. "No. This is Cora we're talking about."

"Cora's the daughter I always wanted. I would do anything to protect her. You handled the people who hurt her, correct?" He looked between Renato and me.

Renato nodded. "Yes."

"Then we move on and figure out how to coexist with

the Vargas Cartel. The bloodshed connected to our name is not good for our family."

"You did what you had to do years ago with Amadias Vargas, but now you want me to step aside like a little puppy?"

Father's mouth tightened. "I would do anything to protect my children. It's time we talked rather than continued to kill."

"That's a risk," Renato chimed in.

"Exactly. We look the other way, and they move in on more of our territory."

Father fiddled with his pen. "Go home and be with Cora. I'll set up a meeting between you and Enrique."

"The only way I'll see that asshole is in a body bag." I glared at my father. If I didn't know any better, I'd suspect a villain was creeping into my family. "I need to go."

"EJ, do as I say."

I stood and headed for the door. "And if I don't?"

"I may be retired, but you will not disrespect me."

Being named after my father came with more responsibility than my brothers. He expected me to be like him in every way. Yes, I'd left Cora for the family business, but my mind was my own.

I left the house and headed back to my place to talk to Cora. We needed to figure out how we were going to move forward. I couldn't stay away from her anymore. And I wouldn't have rules put into place about how she and I interacted around my family.

* * *

I slipped through the house and reset the alarm. Dropping my keys and wallet on the side table near the door, I marched down the hall, noticing Cora asleep on the couch. I released a sigh and bent to pick her up. She squirmed in my arms, and her eyes blinked open in confusion. I climbed the stairs to my bedroom, kicked the door open, and placed her on the bed. Cora slid up to the headboard and tucked a lock of her hair behind her ear,

I moved away and stood against the dresser to face her. "We need to talk."

Cora inhaled raggedly. "I know."

"I texted you."

Cora tucked her feet underneath her. "I'm not sure where my phone is."

"I'm sorry I wasn't there for you."

"Me too."

"Whatever happened between us, I thought you knew I was the one person you could always count on."

"EJ—"

"No, Cora. You knew how I'd react to the miscarriage."

"You hurt me badly, EJ. I didn't trust you anymore."

I raked a hand through my hair. "We were both so young, and you needed to focus on school."

Cora pushed off the headboard. "I would've stuck with you when you joined the cartel."

"And have your mother hate me for when you got hurt or for not pursuing your dreams." I scoffed. "This is no life for you. I thought you deserved better."

"I make my own decisions about my future." She pointed from herself to me.

"Was your mother with you when you ...?" I let my words trail off.

"Yes," she whispered.

"Shit. I wish I'd known."

"It's over now, EJ."

"You don't have to worry about the robbery."

Her eyes ballooned wide. "Did you kill them?"

"Like I said, nothing for you to worry about anymore."

"Thank you. But busting into my place of business doesn't work for me, EJ."

I smirked. "Cora, you've always been my business, and that will never change, even if you went to live in another country. I would still know your every move."

"I didn't know Enrique and you knew each other."

My glare returned. "He's using you to get to me."

"What do you mean?"

"We have evidence of Enrique and the guy who robbed you together. Everything was planned out weeks, probably months, in advance. Enrique wants revenge against my father. He wants to take over Chicago."

"Does your father know?"

I nodded. "Just left him, and he wants me to leave it alone."

"Maybe you should."

"Cora, you know my brothers and I will never let anyone take what's ours."

Cora sighed and shook her head. "I thought he was a genuine customer."

"Enrique is dangerous."

"Do you think he had anything to do with trying to buy my clinic?"

"Yeah, his brother's name is Izan Cumin Vargas. They hired a law firm as a third party to purchase your place."

Cora propped her elbows on her knees. "Wow."

"He's going to be taken care of soon."

"Good."

"What about us?"

Her eyes lifted to mine. "Do you want the truth?"

I palmed her cheek. "I want you, Cora."

"I think we should date first and see how things go."

I chuckled. "Cora, we've come a long way since we were kids."

I wanted to sink into her tightness right now, but it would have to wait until she was comfortable.

"I agree, but we've changed over the years, and you may not think of me the same way. I'm not the naïve girl you knew back then."

"We've both grown."

"Dating and no sex."

"Cora." I huffed a laugh at her terms.

"Either you agree, or we stay friends."

"I told you in New York we'll never be friends, not after everything we've been through."

Cora's eyes flared with desire, no doubt remembering our hot sex in New York. "That was a one-time thing. We need to get to know each other all over again." She extended her hand. "Hi, I'm Cora."

"You're playing games."

"My way or no way."

I pushed off the wall and took her hand. I brought it to my lips and kissed her knuckles before shaking it. "Hi, Cora. I'm Elio Jr, but you can call me EJ."

"Nice to meet you, EJ."

"Are you hungry?"

"Yes, but I need to get home and shower."

"I have a few of your things here."

"EJ, I refuse to wear one of your little playthings."

"These are clothes I bought for you a while ago to

keep here, along with your favorite shampoo and body wash."

"When?"

"After I saw you at Christmas," I confessed.

"Thank you, but I don't want you buying me things." She stood and made her way down the stairs.

"You don't get to tell me how I spoil you," I said, following her.

"Here we go again. Let's keep it simple and date first."

"We can go on a date, but we're together, Cora." I slipped an arm around her waist, tugged her close, and pressed our lips together. "Perfect." I pulled back and wiped her lipstick off.

Cora gently pushed me away. "No sex or kissing."

"That won't last long." Cora loved sex as much as I did.

"Anissa and I are planning a baby shower for Devi," she said as we headed outside to the car.

I helped Cora into the passenger seat before sliding behind the wheel. "Tell me the cost, and I'll have my mother pay for everything."

"I can pay. I want you to meet my friends."

"There's something else we need to talk about." I started the car.

Cora waited for me to continue. "What now?"

"Might be time for you to move your business elsewhere."

"I like where we are."

"Cora, you need to understand. The Vargas Cartel is going to retaliate."

"I have nothing to do with the cartel on either side."

"You're mine, and they know I'll do anything to protect you."

"I'm not moving."

God, she was stubborn.

Freddie was in the car in front of us, and I continued to check the wing mirror as Cora talked about her plans for the baby shower and me meeting her best friends.

We ordered food and hung out at her place for the rest of the night. I didn't fight her about sleeping in the spare room. I was just happy she wanted to start over.

Chapter 11

Cora

Over the following week, EJ kept his word. He took me out on dates, even with all the craziness with Vargas trying to get revenge.

Devi invited me to go shopping with her, and I asked Rena and Mckayla to join us. Adelina was only too happy to watch the kids. I promised EJ I would call when we were done.

I picked up a hat in Macy's and checked the price tag. I tried it on and posed in the mirror.

"EJ told us you've been hanging out lately," Mckayla said.

I smiled and shrugged my shoulders. "He and I are friends."

"Friends?"

"Yes, friends who used to date."

Rena picked up a large floppy hat and tried it on. "Dated and almost had a child."

Devi sat down and waited for the sales associate to bring her shoes. "Do you believe you're ready for a relationship as adults?"

"He knows I want to take things slow."

"Has Enrique come around?"

"No, thank God. EJ's down my throat about selling my vet clinic."

"He told Renato that he wanted you to move closer to Calabresi holdings."

"My goal is to be accessible to everyone, regardless of finances. Moving closer to their building would draw me into a more expensive business situation."

"EJ has the money. He can help you."

"I've never wanted EJ to take care of me."

"Not taking care of you. He knows you want to be an independent businesswoman."

"I understand the cartel life. It makes the women dependent on the men."

"Mckayla and I still work outside of the cartel. It's not like the old school of mob life, Cora," Rena pointed out.

"I need to keep something for myself, away from the Calabresi name."

"Fair enough. If you love him, take your time," Devi advised.

Mckayla was talking with Savio on the phone, so I walked toward the makeup section with Jason following behind.

"Jason, you can stay with the girls. I'm five feet away,"

"Boss wants us with you at all times."

I grinned mischievously and crossed my fingers. "I promise I won't run off like I did in New York."

"I'm watching you," Jason stated.

I chortled and headed to the makeup aisle. "Yes, boss."

The sales associate greeted me as I picked up a dark red lipstick to try.

"That line is the most popular right now," the sales associate told me.

I looked in the mirror. "It goes on smoothly. I like the color." Something caught my eye on the escalator, and I dropped the lipstick on the counter.

"Is there something else you'd like to try?"

"Uh, not right now." I walked around the counter and headed toward the escalator. Enrique was there with a phone up to his ear. We were being followed again. I needed to warn Jason.

Before I could follow him, a hand grabbed me from behind.

"Cora, I thought that was you."

I turned to see Anissa's boyfriend. "Mitchel! Hey, what are you doing here?"

He lifted the bag in his hand. "Getting a gift for Anissa."

I looked around. "Is she here?"

"She's at work. Everything okay with you?"

"Fine, I just thought I saw someone."

"Cora, are you okay?" Jason asked, appearing behind Mitchel.

"I'm fine. Mitchel is a friend."

Mitchel extended a hand, but Jason ignored him.

I smiled at Mitchel. "Tell Anissa I'll call her later."

I left him with a small wave and pulled my phone from my pocket to call EJ.

"Cora?" he answered immediately.

"I just saw him."

"Saw who?"

"Enrique Vargas."

"Where?"

"Leaving the mall."

"Have Jason drop you off to me."

"I have work to do."

"Your staff can function without you for a day or two."

Devi, Rena, and Mckayla joined me.

"Hey, you okay?" Devi asked.

"Let me call you back." I hung up on EJ and slipped the phone into my pocket.

"You look like you've seen a ghost," Rena muttered.

"Are you guys ready to go?"

"Sure. I invited the girls to my baby shower," Devi announced.

"When is it?" Mckayla tossed a piece of gum in her mouth.

"In a month."

I looked around the parking lot for Enrique's vehicle as Jason helped us into the car. He slid behind the wheel with Enuoe in the passenger seat.

"What's going on, Cora? You're freaking me out," Devi said.

"Nothing. I saw Mitchel," I bluffed.

"Anissa's boyfriend?"

"Yeah, he had to grab something for her."

Rena and Mckayla didn't seem to buy my answer.

Jason dropped Devi's home first. I kissed her on the cheek, and Enuoe carried her bags into the house. I waved goodbye as Enuoe returned to the car, and we continued to drop the other ladies off.

"Adelina wants to come to the shower," Rena said, her phone in her hand.

I nodded. "That's fine."

"Great. I know she wants to get her a gift."

"She'll love that," I murmured distractedly. My mind was still on seeing Enrique at the mall.

We dropped Rena and Mckayla home, and a few minutes later, we arrived at EJ's office. I held up my hand to stall Jason as he went to help me get out of the car. Making my way through the security line, I picked up a visitor's badge. I last came here a few years ago for lunch with Vincenzo.

I slipped in behind the last person on the elevator and pushed the button for the top floor. A minute later, the doors opened, and a few people got off.

Vincenzo stepped into the elevator as the doors started to close. "Cora! What are you doing here?" he asked, hugging me.

"I came to see your brother."

The elevator stopped on EJ's floor, and Vincenzo let me off first. "He might still be in a meeting."

"I can wait in his office."

I looked around as people ran back and forth in a rush. "Why is everyone stressed?"

"We just landed a big real estate deal."

"Congrats."

"Thanks. You seem a little distracted, Cora."

I took a seat on the couch in EJ's office. "There's a lot going on."

"What are you doing in my office?" EJ asked as he entered the room.

"Cora and I ran into each other on the elevator," Vincenzo explained.

EJ tossed some papers onto his desk, marched toward me, and bent to capture my lips.

I pecked him on the mouth. "Remember the rules."

"I've never followed the rules." EJ winked at me.

"Are we going out to dinner?"

"Yes, I just need to sign some papers."

"Where are we going?"

"Surprise."

I scanned down at my shorts and T-shirt. "Surprise? I'm not dressed for a surprise."

"You look beautiful."

"I told you to keep it simple."

"I asked you out for a date. I'll spoil you how I want," EJ stated.

"Can I go home to change?"

EJ smiled. "Check the closet."

I jumped up and opened the closet to see a light blue dress hanging on the back of the door.

"Where did you pick up this dress?"

EJ smirked. "I can't tell you all my secrets."

I shook my head and huffed as I went into the bathroom to get changed. I decided to wait until after the date to tell him about Enrique. It would only piss him off. Twenty minutes later, I left the bathroom to find EJ on the phone. I turned my back for him to zip me up.

"Keep me updated," EJ said to the person on the other end of the line before hanging up.

"I'm ready to go," I said, holding the clothes I'd changed out of.

"You can drop those in the trash," EJ said.

"These are my favorite shorts."

"I can buy you more shorts, Cora." EJ took the clothes from my hands and tossed them in the trash bin.

"EJ—"

He tugged me close and lifted my hand to his lips, pressing a kiss to my knuckles.

"Are you going to tell me where you're taking me?"

"I told you, it's a surprise."

EJ locked his office door and told his staff he'd be out for the rest of the day before we took the private elevator to the lobby.

* * *

After a few hours of shopping, hanging out together, and talking, we drove through the streets of Chicago in the early morning. I checked the time to see it was three am. The sun was setting as we left the city, and I began worrying as I saw a sign for a private airport.

I looked at EJ as he typed on his phone. "I hope you're not kidnapping me again."

He winked. "One night."

"Tell me where you're taking me?"

"To dinner."

I groaned. "EJ."

We exited the car, and EJ reached for my hand, laughing softly at my sour expression. "I'm taking you to Paris."

My mouth dropped open in shock. "Paris, *France*?"

"Yes," he replied, rubbing the goosebumps on my arm.

I couldn't comprehend his words. "For dinner?'

"Yes, Cora. One night in Paris for dinner."

"What about the stuff going on with Enrique?"

"I'm handling it. Nothing for you to worry about."

The wind tousled my hair as the private jet stairs lowered. EJ was surprising me more and more.

I climbed the stairs and made my way to the seats to see a tray of champagne and fruit waiting. "Is this a joke?"

"No. We're spending time together with no interruptions. I want to show you that I'm here for you," EJ said as we settled into our seats.

"This is a new EJ Calabresi."

"I want to earn you, Cora. I want to show you that our mistakes are in the past." He captured my lips, and I wound my arms around his neck.

As the jet took off, EJ's phone rang. He ignored it, quickly sending a text before turning it off. I snuggled up next to him and closed my eyes.

Hours later, I was woken by kisses along my cheeks and lips. I opened my eyes and smiled sleepily at EJ.

"We're here."

"Paris." I stretched my arms and yawned. It was dark outside the window, but I could make out three Escalades lined up on the tarmac. "Are they all for us?"

"You're my priority. You'll never go without protection."

I stood on my tiptoes and brushed my lips against his. EJ gripped my ass and pressed his hard girth against me as we made out. He stopped us from going further, patting my butt as we exited the plane. We climbed into the middle car and headed to dinner. It didn't take long to arrive at the restaurant, which looked empty from the street.

"Are you sure they're open?" I asked as I climbed out of the car behind him.

"Positive. I rented the entire place."

"For just the two of us?"

He linked our hands and guided me into the restaurant. Staff waited, lined up with smiles on their faces.

"Mr. Calabresi, your table is ready," the hostess said with a warm smile.

Lights twinkled around the restaurant, and a picture

of a pier was lit up on the wall. The chairs were gilded, and all the round tables held flowers and candles. The walls were clad with warm wood panels, and there was a piano in the corner. The whole place oozed romance.

I removed my jacket and placed it on the back of the chair as EJ pulled it out for me. "Thank you for this," I murmured as I sat.

EJ sat opposite me and reached for my hand. "I wanted to be alone with you so we could talk away from family and friends."

I twirled the wine in my glass.

"I fucked up years ago. I've learned that if I want something, I have to make my intentions known, and I want you, Cora."

"Want me in the sense of me going along with what you say?"

"I hurt you, and I apologize, but you can't hold that over me forever."

I scoffed at his statement. "I don't."

"You do. I'm not trying to start a fight, but we need to come to terms with our past so we can move forward. You're mine, Cora. If anyone tries to get between us, I won't hesitate to hurt them."

"Threatening people isn't how this works, EJ."

Our server brought our food and placed it on the table. I thanked her and picked up my fork to start eating.

"I want you to consider moving your vet clinic," EJ said.

"I've only agreed to date you, and you're already making demands."

"We dated at fourteen. It's different now. You're my woman, and I'm your man."

"So you're just going to skip over what I want?"

"What do you want?"

I sat back in my seat and stared at him. "I want you to court me and not take over my life with cartel bullshit."

EJ topped up my wine glass. "My life is complicated. You know I can't leave the family business, so you need to be able to handle that."

Could I handle that? "You expect me to be a yes person and not question you, correct?"

"Cora, I know you, and you know me. Never in our relationship have I expected you to do as I say."

"Great. So long as you know I'm not Mckayla, Rena, or Sonya. Our relationship is not like your brothers'. I plan on working and having my friends."

"Anything else?"

"I apologize for keeping the miscarriage a secret."

"Thank you."

"We can try again."

"Happy you're giving me a second chance."

"Sex is still not on the table."

He looked at me with lust in his eyes.

"Don't look at me like that."

EJ pulled my chair next to his and kissed me on the neck. I met his lips, and we made out like we were teenagers again, only this time, we didn't have to worry about our parents finding out.

I was vaguely aware of the server arriving with our desserts. She cleared her throat awkwardly before retreating hastily.

"We should eat dessert," I whispered against his lips.

EJ trailed his hand up my thigh and nibbled on my ear. "I want a different kind of dessert."

I moaned and gripped his wrist as he slipped his hand under my dress. "EJ, we can't."

"Why, Cora? What are you afraid of?" EJ gazed into my eyes, and memories of our first kiss played in my mind.

I turned my head, slid my tongue into his mouth, and drowned in his touch.

EJ wrapped his hand gently around my throat. I opened my legs slightly, feeling the warmth of his finger as it hovered over my panties.

"Stop fighting us and give yourself to me," EJ muttered.

"Yes," I panted.

Chapter 12

Elio Jr

I kicked the hotel door closed behind us. I looked into Cora's eyes, remembering how our first kiss took my breath away when we were teenagers. I stalked around her like a predator, slipping her dress from her shoulders and peppering kisses along her neck and behind her ear. Her soft skin sent a fire blazing along my spine. I wanted to drop to my knees and show her how much I'd worshiped and loved her from the moment we'd met.

This reconnection wouldn't stop once we left Paris. I planned to show Cora my world, how I'd never stopped loving her, even while we were apart.

I cupped her breast in one hand, slipping the other between her thighs and over her warm pussy.

"Are you wet for me?" I teased the seam of her panties with my fingers.

"Yes," she cooed.

"Open some more, baby."

On my command, her legs spread wider, and she

squeezed her eyes shut. "EJ, please stop teasing." The need in her voice told me she was ready for me.

"You won't be running out this time," I growled in her ear, tugging her head back and smacking her pussy.

Cora moaned, and her juices ran down her leg. I turned her to face the bed and pushed her to lie on her stomach. I quickly removed my clothes, and jolts of pleasure ran through me as I remembered our night in New York. I drank in her perfect form, planning to devour every inch before we returned home.

Rubbing her ass cheek, I smacked it sharply, and Cora cried out. I ran my rod along her slit and pushed my way in, stopping before I released too early. I hadn't been with her in a few months and wanted our time to last.

"Oh, God," Cora groaned.

I pumped my hips slowly to draw out the pleasure. "I plan on fucking you all night, Cora."

"Baby, I need you," she whimpered.

My dick grew even harder at her pleas, and my raw grunts filled the room. I thrust faster, driven on by the sensation of Cora's slick pussy. I wanted to make her squirt like she used to when we were together.

"Have you been with anyone else, Cora?"

She shook her head. "No. Oh, God!"

"God won't help you if I find out Enrique touched you." Only Cora instilled this kind of jealousy within me.

I pulled out of her tight sheath. "Turn around."

Cora fell to her knees and crawled toward me on all fours. Before I could do anything, she shoved my hands away, gripped my dick, and took me in her mouth.

"Goddamn, baby."

Nothing about this was sweet and proper with Cora.

She released me with a pop, spit on the tip, and spread it around, mixing it with my pre-cum. I glared at her, wondering who she'd learned this from. She smirked and took me back in her mouth, right to the back of her throat.

"Fuck. Don't play with me, Cora," I grunted.

"I don't play games, EJ. Now, fuck me."

I pushed her on her back, spread her legs wide, and pushed inside her. We both moaned at the exquisite sensation.

She shivered as I pulled out and thrust back in over and over. "Mmm...Yes, EJ. Keep going."

Her eyes rolled back in her head as her tight walls squeezed me. Her screams of passion and the sound of our bodies slapping together were a symphony to my ears.

"You're so fucking beautiful like this, baby."

My head fell back, and my spine stiffened as we both came. I slumped on top of her, out of breath but ready for the next round. Her hungry lips met mine, and she hooked her leg around my waist. She arched her back, and we continued to fuck like long-lost lovers in a Hollywood movie.

* * *

Cora and I talked for hours on the plane ride back to Chicago. We had sex on the private jet, and I promised we'd return to Paris for a longer vacation. I vowed to communicate better, and she promised to let me know if Enrique or any of his men came around again. At first, I wanted to tell her to stop working, but it would lead to more arguing, and she'd always been independent.

When I arrived home, I showered and slept for a few hours before Savio summoned me to a meeting.

"We've come here under difficult circumstances," Cacho began. Enrique and Izan sat smugly on either side of him, waiting to piss me off. The city was under their thumb, and we needed to move silently to find out as much as possible about their plans.

"Difficult is navigating New York traffic. Your family is trying to stake a claim on something that doesn't belong to them," Savio stated.

Enrique whispered in his brother's ear.

"We can negotiate a price," Cacho said.

My jaw clenched at the bullshit coming out of Cacho's mouth regarding a truce between his family and mine. He thought we were only about the money, but our family was about respect. Even my father knew peace couldn't happen without respect. Cacho offering money set off warning bells in my head.

I shook my head. "Money is off the table."

"Then we do whatever we want," Enrique threatened.

"You can try," I replied, leaning back in my chair.

Enrique smirked. "How's our girl?"

Enrique had crossed a line by involving Cora. "Try all you want. Cora's out of your league."

"She's exactly what I need next to me in Mexico," Enrique responded.

That pissed me off. I reached under the table and pulled out my gun.

"We didn't come here for that." Cacho gripped his brother's arm to hold him back.

The gun sat at my side. "Keep Cora's name out of your mouth."

Enrique glanced from the gun to me. He removed his gun and laid it on the table. "You six feet under and Cora grieving in my arms."

The tension in the room was tangible as both families waited to see who would make the first move.

Izan tapped Enrique, sensing the tension could explode into full-out gunfire if they didn't leave. They stood, and I followed to ensure they left our property. Before I could react, Enrique landed a punch to my face.

I reeled back, clasping my jaw and shaking it off. "Is that all you got?" I growled.

I launched myself at him, and my fist hit his face with a satisfying crunch. It caused a ripple effect, and everybody around me started to fight. The Vargas Cartel guards charged at Savio as Enrique raised his gun. A red haze descended before my eyes. I grabbed his wrist, and the gun went off, causing everyone to scatter.

I wrestled the gun from his grasp. "Leave while you can," I shouted.

Enrique's swiped the blood from his eye and motioned for his brothers to leave with him, "You have no idea how ugly we can get," he threatened.

"Stay away from Cora!" I yelled to his retreating back.

"He's not going down easy," Savio remarked, staring after him.

I didn't care. I was prepared to die for what was mine.

"You good?" Renato asked, wrapping his arm around my shoulders as we made our way out to the cars.

I looked at my fist covered in blood. "Cora's going to be pissed at me for making her stay at my place."

"To protect her from Enrique," Renato pointed out.

"She's going to fight me. She'll think I'm trying to control her."

"Talk to her and see if she can stay with our parents," Savio suggested as I climbed into the back seat. He slid in next to me as Freddie started the car.

"Clean up the place and get rid of the tapes," I directed Renato.

"Ah, the life of an Enforcer," Renato sighed, shutting the door and tapping his palm on the roof.

"I need to run by Cora's place to let her know," I told Savio as Freddie drove toward the city.

* * *

I pushed the buzzer on Cora's front door. I had a key, but she didn't know that which would annoy her. The door opened to reveal Cora casually dressed in a shirt and shorts, with her hair in a ponytail.

I reached out and wrapped my hand around her waist, drawing her to me as my mouth crashed down on hers. I backed her into the apartment and kicked the door shut.

Cora pulled back and smiled at me. "This is a nice surprise."

I licked my lips. "Why are you opening the door dressed like this?"

Cora scanned her clothes. "What's wrong with the way I'm dressed?"

"Answering the door in these sexy little shorts," I growled, trailing my fingers along her thigh.

I took her hand and tugged her to sit on the couch, settling her in my lap.

"What happened to your hand?" she exclaimed when she saw my bruised knuckles.

"Nothing to worry about."

"EJ, tell me the truth."

I stretched my hand out. "My fist met with Enrique's face again."

"Should I be worried?"

"No. He knows to stay away from you. What would you say if I asked you to move in with me?"

"No."

"Why not?"

"EJ, we just got back together."

"And?"

"Let me grab a Band-Aid to clean you up."

"Cora, I'm serious. This is getting dangerous," I rasped.

"I hear you, EJ. But Enrique doesn't know where I live."

"Cora, you know better than anyone that if he wants to find you, he will."

Cora tugged me to my feet and guided me to the bedroom. She disappeared into the bathroom and returned with a first aid kit. Sitting on the bed, she removed the alcohol wipes and indicated that I should sit next to her. I winced as she cleaned the blood from my knuckles before securing a Band-Aid.

"He knows you'll kill him if he so much as breathes in my direction," Cora said quietly.

"Doesn't matter. I want you with me at my place."

She rose from the bed. "No."

I gripped her arm. "He's using you to get to me."

"You think I don't know that?"

"So why won't you listen to me?"

"I refuse to stop working and living my life, EJ. Do what you need to do, but my independence is important." She returned to the bathroom, and I heard her slam the first aid kit on the counter.

I sighed, deciding to change the subject—for now. "How are the baby shower plans coming along?"

"Fine. Anissa has everything lined up."

"If anything odd happens, I won't hesitate to lock you in my room," I joked as she returned to the bedroom.

"Yes, sir." Cora wrapped her arms around my neck and gave me a quick kiss.

I sifted my fingers through her hair. "I need to get to the office and finish up some paperwork."

"Okay."

"Come with me."

"I have to go into the clinic."

"Right now?" I looked at my watch to see it was almost two in the afternoon.

Cora moved away and walked to her closet. "A few dog appointments."

Being close to Cora again made me happy. If anyone came between us, I would go to the ends of the earth to destroy them.

Cora laid a pair of black slacks and a white silk shirt on the bed. She slipped off her shirt, revealing her bare breasts.

"You're teasing me," I groaned, reaching out to pinch her nipple.

"I have work, and you need to get to the office." Cora opened the drawer and grabbed a bra.

"The office can wait." I nudged her back onto the bed and climbed on top of her. Dipping my hand between her legs, I slicked my finger through her folds and brought it to my lips. I extended my finger for her to taste.

She shook her head. "Later. You can stop by and finish what you just started."

I moaned and fell onto my side, watching as she finished dressing. "At least let me drop you off at the office."

"Nope. I see what you're trying to do, EJ, and it won't work."

I followed her out of the bedroom to the front door. "What am I doing?"

"If you drop me off, that means you get to pick me up."

"Baby, I need you safe."

She patted my cheek. "I will take every precaution."

"I'll be calling every hour, and if you don't answer, expect me to show up at your place."

"Okay," she sighed. "Dinner and a movie later?"

"Sounds good." I walked Cora to her car, watching her settle in the driver's seat and buckle up.

She drove off with Jason following behind in his car. Her safety was my priority, and if I had to go behind her back to ensure it, I would. Enrique had made his intentions clear, but I would be a step ahead.

* * *

"Repeat that," I barked down the phone at Renato.

"I retrieved footage from the mall in New York. Seems Izan bumped into Cora there before she left to return to Chicago."

"So she's been on their radar for a while." I was in the car on my way back to the office. Savio wanted me to review and sign off on some paperwork before we broke ground on the new property. He wanted to open hotels with the Calabresi name so we appeared more legit in the media.

"Send me the footage, Renato."

"Are you on your way to the office?"

"Yeah."

"I'll meet you there."

Hanging up, I gritted my teeth at how close Cora had come to being taken by the enemy. I wasn't waiting on a truce like my father. The Vargas Cartel would move back to Mexico, or blood would be shed.

Freddie pulled up outside the office. I climbed out and went through the security. I took the private elevator, watching the numbers ascend until I reached my floor. Stepping out, I headed straight to Renato's office. He was sitting with Savio behind his desk.

"Show me," I said immediately.

Renato turned the computer around, and I watched the video of Cora bumping into Izan at the mall.

"Play it again."

They were calculated; I'd give them that. But they made a mistake in thinking we were soft and would let anything fly when it came to our family.

"He's a dead man," I stated.

"We can take care of him tonight." Renato agreed.

"If you do this, it will cause blowback," Savio warned.

"Fuck blowback. I'm ready to end them all," I snarled, glancing between Savio and Renato.

Chapter 13

Cora

"**W**ake up, *bella*." Warm hands ran up my thighs, and soft lips caressed my skin. EJ came over to my place late, and we had dinner and fell asleep right after. I was too exhausted from work to stay awake long enough to watch a movie.

I slowly opened my eyes and turned onto my back. "Morning," I mumbled groggily.

"I made you breakfast."

I smiled at his accomplishment. Usually, my mother or Adelina cooked at their home when he was growing up. "When did you start cooking?"

EJ placed a hand on his chest in mock hurt. "I had a great teacher. Her name is Marilyn."

"My mother taught you to cook? When?" I lifted my hand to cup my head against the headboard.

"Years ago, while you were at college."

"What can you cook?"

"Simple things. But I made you breakfast, and we need to talk."

"Not about me working again, EJ."

"No, it's about New York."

He stood, and my eyes moved over his muscular body. He was only wearing boxers, and his thick girth poked for attention.

"What are you staring at?" he asked.

I sighed. "You're beautiful."

"So are you, baby. Come and eat."

I tossed the covers back and climbed out of bed. Pulling on my robe, I quickly freshened up in the bathroom before sauntering to the kitchen. The table was laden with brioche, French toast, coffee, fruit, and oatmeal.

EJ pulled out my chair and then sat beside me. I picked up my glass of orange juice and took a sip. EJ placed a napkin on his lap and grabbed my hand.

"You were distracted last night. Did something happen?"

"You made contact with Izan Vargas in New York."

I frowned. "No, I didn't. I was with you the entire time."

"When you went to the mall and escaped."

"I had Jason and Freddie with me."

"Think back. You bumped into someone."

I folded my arms and sat back in the chair. "The guy in the grey suit?"

"Enrique's brother is a lawyer for the Vargas Cartel."

"So what are you saying?"

"They've been following you the entire time to get to me and our family."

"A setup?"

"Yeah. We watched the video from the mall."

"But—"

EJ leaned in to kiss me on the forehead. "I'm taking care of him."

"Please don't get in trouble, EJ."

"Can't avoid that."

EJ was all business when it came to his family, but he was just as capable of turning into a menacing mobster like Renato.

"Do you want this forever, Cora?"

His question gave me pause. Forever with EJ made me think of marriage and kids. *Was the long break worth the wait? He's different now, Cora.*

"I do," I whispered.

"Then it will all be fine."

"Are you going to kill him?"

"You know the answer to that."

I moved to straddle his lap. "Be careful. Maybe you can meditate."

"Too late for that."

His tone was too calm. I was worried he wouldn't be the same EJ after all the cartel fighting.

"Just promise me to think before you push yourself over the cliff."

He focused on my lips and then my eyes. "Anything pertaining to you drives me overboard."

"Come to the baby shower with me."

EJ grasped my thighs and lowered his head to my chest. "No."

"Please. All my friends will have their boyfriends and husbands with them."

"Will that make you happy?"

"Yes, it will."

"Who's pregnant?"

"Devi."

"Fine. Don't expect me to dress up."

I chuckled and smashed our lips together, sucking on his bottom lip. He pulled me in tighter and squeezed my ass, grinding me against his erection.

I pulled away reluctantly. "I need to get ready for work."

"Call me when you get there and when you leave."

I smirked. "Mr. Bossy is back."

I slid out of his lap, picked up my coffee, and returned to the bedroom to get dressed for work.

* * *

I shut the cabinet after restocking the supplies in the storage room. Returning to my office with lunch ordered from my favorite restaurant, I took a seat to file some paperwork. The day was already half over. We'd had back-to-back appointments with sick animals. I paused to check my text messages.

Anissa: *The venue is organized for the shower.*

Me: *Make sure we have enough food.*

Anissa: *The catering company knows it's intimate. About fifty people.*

Me: *I sent the invitations out.*

Anissa: *Mitchel finally said he would come.*

Me: *I forgot to tell you I saw him at the mall.*

Anissa: *He never told me.*

Me: *lol! He's a guy. They never remember.*

Anissa: *True.*

I closed out the text messages and finished some

reports before scheduling appointments for the next week. Once I was done, I turned off my computer and gathered my bag and purse. I waved goodbye to Julia and Colson, who were talking with customers at the front desk.

Head down, I scrabbled in my purse, looking for my car keys, and barreled straight into a hard body. Stumbling back, I looked up to see Enrique with an evil smirk on his face.

"We keep running into each other."

"Leave me alone."

Enrique stepped closer.

I glanced around the street. "I have guards here."

"Really? Where?" Enrique motioned to the truck Enuoe drove. He was motionless in the driver's seat, a single bullet hole between his eyes.

"You killed him!" I gasped.

Enrique leaned into my ear and whispered, "Tell your boyfriend we're coming."

"Get away from me." I reached into my pocket for my phone and hit speed dial to call EJ before it was knocked from my hand.

"Oh, dear. You seem to have dropped your phone," a voice said behind me.

I spun to face the other man. "Stay away from me!"

"I don't believe you've met my brother, Izan," Enrique said casually.

"Cora!" I heard EJ's voice through the phone.

"EJ!"

Izan lifted his foot and stomped on my phone, smashing it into pieces. He advanced on me and pushed me against their car. "He can't save you, princess."

The evil intent in his eyes caused my blood to freeze

in my veins. His phone rang, and he pulled it out of his pocket. The name scrolling across the screen caused my throat to tighten with fear. Using his momentary distraction, I shoved him with all my strength and took off back to my office, bursting inside and slamming and locking the door behind me.

"Cora, are you all right?" Colson asked urgently.

Adrenaline pumped through my body. "Call the police."

"What happened?" Julia looked scared.

Gunfire exploded. Julia and I screamed as we dropped to the ground.

"Cora!"

"EJ!" I jumped up and ran for the door, unlocking it and throwing it open. I leaped into his arms with a sob.

"It's okay. I've got you, baby." EJ wiped the tears from my eyes.

He half-carried me outside to the car. Nausea churned in my stomach at seeing Izan's dead body before EJ moved to block him from view.

"You're going to my parent's place," EJ said once I was secure in the back of his town car.

"He's dead," I whispered through numb lips.

Usually, I was protected from this side of the family business, but now I'd seen it up close and personal. Nothing could have prepared me for being thrust into EJ's cartel business.

"He's ... dead," I repeated.

Distraught, I fell into EJ's arms, and he held me close until we reached his family home. My legs were wobbly as he helped me out of the car. As I entered the house, my mother ran toward me with a sob.

"Cora, why are you crying?" She gathered me in her arms, smoothing her hand over my hair.

"I can't breathe."

Mom kissed my cheek. "Calm down and talk to me."

I felt suffocated and needed some air. "He's dead."

EJ moved behind me. "We need to have a family meeting."

"EJ, what happened?" Adelina asked, appearing behind Marilyn.

"Izan Vargas is dead. They killed Enuoe, and I killed Izan," EJ announced.

Adelina frowned. "What does that mean?"

"It means we're at war," EJ replied grimly.

"Cora needs to stay here," Adelina said firmly.

I shook my head. "I'm not hiding."

Adelina passed me a tissue, and I wiped my nose and eyes.

"Enrique won't stop until he has you," EJ reminded me.

"Maybe you should stay here, honey," Mom said worriedly. I hated that she'd been pulled into EJ's business and was scared for me.

"Let me think it over. I have Devi's baby shower."

EJ demanded. "Cancel it."

"I'm not canceling her baby shower."

"It's not safe, Cora," EJ snapped.

"Nothing is safe with any of you!" I yelled.

I threw up my hands and stomped to the kitchen, pacing the floor.

"Cora."

My head snapped up at the calm voice. "Mr. Calabresi."

He smiled. "How many times have I told you to call me Elio."

"Hard to do that when your son is named after you," I said, trying to return his smile.

Elio Sr. chuckled as he handed me a glass of water. "We only want to keep you safe, Cora."

"It's too much. One second, he was trying to grab me, and the next, he was dead."

"Izan tried to hurt you."

"I know what you all do, but it just became very real."

"Can you accept EJ as a husband with his life in the cartel?"

I placed a hand on my stomach, fighting nausea.

"Adelina grew around the business, and she still had a hard time with the things I had to do."

"If you could've chosen a different path, would you?"

Elio Sr. looked thoughtful. "Maybe. But it's a moot point now. My boys have grown up in this life and know what's expected of them."

"Cora."

I turned to see EJ standing in the doorway.

"You all right?"

I cleared my throat and nodded. "Can we talk about this later?"

EJ walked toward me and reached for my hand.

"Food is ready." Adelina came around the corner.

Elio Sr.'s eyes lit up as he saw his wife. I hoped EJ and I would be the same when we were older.

"Come and try to eat something, Cora. It will help to settle your stomach," Adelina said knowingly. She linked her arm with mine and led me to the dining room.

* * *

"Breaking news. Izan Vargas, a major drug cartel player, was found dead today."

Rena took the remote from me and turned off the TV before sitting beside me on the couch. "Watching the news reports will only make you relive it," she said softly.

Mckayla entered the room and sat on my other side, taking my hand in hers.

"I shouldn't feel guilty, but I do."

"Izan knew the risk when he approached you," Rena said.

"Will there be a war?"

Mckayla nodded. "Yes. Once you cross the family, death is the only answer."

My head fell back on the couch, and I closed my eyes. "A regular day at work turning into a crime scene."

"It was lucky no one else was hurt," Rena muttered.

I sighed. "You're right." Izan had left the business cards about buying the clinic. It had all been a ruse to get me out of the way and hurt the Calabresi family.

"How about you take some time away from work and focus on you and EJ? Maybe take a vacation."

"I won't run out on the business."

"I know you want your independence, but your safety comes first, Cora," Mckayla challenged.

"Maybe in a few weeks."

"Think it over, and don't be mad at EJ."

Was I mad at him? He'd killed someone in broad daylight.

"I'm going home."

"You can sleep here tonight."

I stood and headed for the door. "I need my bed, and I have to get ready for the baby shower this weekend."

"Well, keep us updated if you need us." Rena walked alongside me.

"I will, and thank you for listening."

"We're sisters for life." Mckayla and I reached for each other and hugged.

I stared out of the window on the ride home. I could let them win or show I wasn't to be pushed around.

Chapter 14

Elio Jr

The day before.

"EJ!" Cora screamed.

"Cora!" My heart hammered as I heard Izan Vargas in the background. I hung up and dialed Enuoe's number, but it went straight to voicemail.

The door busted open to Freddie and Vincenzo.

"Is she all right?"

"I don't know."

"Izan and Enrique went to her work," Vincenzo said, his phone to his ear.

We rushed out of the office to the private elevator.

"Renato will meet you there," Vincenzo said, putting the phone on speaker.

"We're almost there!" Renato yelled.

The elevator took forever to reach the main lobby. We sprinted from the building, and I slid into the passenger seat beside Freddie.

"Get the clean-up crew to meet us," I told Vincenzo as Freddie put the car in drive and sped out of the parking lot. I tried Cora's number again, but there was no answer.

I called the clinic's landline. "Nobody's picking up. Fuck!"

Cars honked as Freddie drove through red lights. I'd gladly pay the speeding tickets were no doubt accumulating so long as we reached Cora in time.

The next few minutes felt like an hour. We reached the clinic to see Izan and Enrique rushing toward the building. Cora was nowhere in sight. I pulled my gun from the glove compartment as Freddie squealed to a halt. Izan spotted me as I jumped out, and his eyes ballooned wide as I pulled the trigger.

Screams punctured the air from passersby as Izan's body hit the ground. Enrique bellowed with rage and charged toward me, but his men hauled him back and pushed him into their waiting car. They took off with a squeal of tires.

I sprinted toward the clinic and banged on the door. "Cora!"

"EJ!"

I turned to Renato as he appeared behind me. "Enrique got away. Find that motherfucker now!"

I tucked my gun away as the door was wrenched open, and Cora threw herself into my arms. "It's okay. I've got you, baby."

Present Time.

"You killed Izan Vargas," Father said.

I sipped my bourbon. "Yes, but Enrique got away."

"Has he retaliated?"

"No, but he will."

"How far are you planning on taking this, son?"

"They tried to hurt Cora. The only option is retribution."

"We need to hit their businesses," Renato said.

I liked the idea of forcing them into the open. "We know they're still supplying in the Eastside."

Renato nodded. "Maybe send some of our guys up there."

"Keep it under control. I know you won't listen when it comes to Cora, but think first," my father cautioned.

"Enrique should have thought first." I slammed my glass on the desk and stalked out of his office.

I'd stayed at Cora's place last night and texted her earlier to check on her. Leaving Cora's bed was hard. She was still adamant about going ahead with the baby shower for Devi. I planned to increase security in and outside of the venue.

Following Renato's mindset, I took matters into our own hands and headed for Vargas territory. Hit them before they hit us.

"Check them out." Renato pointed at the two men standing on the corner huddled together.

"Pull up on them." I slipped my gun out of my pocket.

"This could get ugly," Renato stated.

"Just sending a message," I said, removing the safety on my gun,

Renato and I were in a used car, a beat-up Honda with stolen tags that would end up in the crusher at a scrap merchant. He revved the gas, and I leaned out the window, putting bullets between the men's eyes. I rolled the window up, and we drove to the next destination four blocks over, where four more men met their fate.

My phone rang with an unknown number as we left the area. I hit answer and brought it to my ear. "Unless you're calling to tell me you're going to fall back, Enrique, get off my phone."

"You're a dead man. You think it's smart to kill my men?"

"Make it easy on yourself and leave."

"No. This is an eye for an eye."

"I'm sure Izan is a sore spot. I understand brother-hood. But you started this."

He chuckled. "She's going to die slowly and painfully after I fuck her."

My hand clenched around the phone. "Try it, and see what happens. I'll come here every day and kill your men."

"And leave your princess alone?"

"She's well protected."

"Only for so long."

"You're going to lose everything, and no one will be able to help you."

I ended the call and slid into my pocket, drumming my fingers against my thigh.

"Enrique?" Renato asked.

I nodded.

"He's running scared."

"He should be."

An hour later, Renato dropped me off at Cora's. I quickly undressed, tossed my clothes in the bathroom hamper, and showered. Cora was still asleep. She'd slept for hours, utterly exhausted from the events at the clinic. Naked, I climbed in beside her, pressing kisses over her forehead and cheeks.

She moaned and planted her hand on my chest. "Where did you go?"

"Business."

"Is it done?"

"Nothing for you to worry about."

Her eyes ran over my face. "What happened?"

"Enrique's pissed about his brother."

"When will we be safe, EJ?"

I cupped her face in my hands. I saw the vulnerability in her eyes. It reminded me of the nineteen-year-old girl who was devastated when we split up. I brushed my lips against hers and slid my tongue into her mouth.

Sliding one hand down her body, I opened her legs and rubbed her clit. Cora opened her legs wider, and I stroked a finger in and out as our mouths danced in sync.

Her nails dug into my back as I eased my erection into her warm, wet pussy. "EJ. Shit..."

I needed her to know I would be her safe place and nothing could break us.

"Fuck, Cora," I groaned as her hot channel milked me. I watched her face scrunch up in ecstasy.

"My God, EJ! It's too much."

"You can take it, baby. You're my world, Cora." I pushed her to the edge with my words and the deep strokes of my cock. Deeper, faster until she was right on the edge.

She twisted her hands in the sheets as I dipped my head and bit her nipple. "Yes! Don't stop, EJ!"

"You ready, baby?"

Her hips lifted to meet my thrusts as I pumped faster, slamming the headboard against the wall. I loved how she gave herself to me to devour.

Cora glared at me as I suddenly pulled out. "No, EJ! Back inside me, please!"

I bent to lick the sweat between her breasts before suckling hard on her nipples, working her to a frenzy.

I lined up with her pussy, tapping the tip against her clit. "You want this, baby?"

"Yes! Please!" she moaned, her hands grasping at me.

I slammed back inside her. "Damn, Cora. You take my breath away."

"Oh! Oh, yes!"

I knew she was about to come. I would be right behind her. "Let go, baby."

"Yes!" She convulsed, pressing her head into the pillow.

I shouted as I followed her over the edge, releasing inside her. I collapsed on top of her as we caught our breath.

* * *

Cora and I had missed the movie the other night, so I ordered takeout, and we headed to my place, which had a theater room. Sante told me he'd keep me updated if anything changed with Enrique and Cacho, so I kept my phone on silent. Tonight was about reassuring Cora we'd be okay.

I put our plates on the table, and our drinks and snacks sat on the bar. Cora curled up next to me with a blanket.

"Work done?" Cora asked, pushing her food around on her plate.

"Renato is taking care of loose ends. Nothing I need to be pulled into right now."

Cora laid her head on my shoulder. "I closed the clinic today. Colson and Julia were scared."

I brushed my lips against hers. "What can I do?"

"You're doing it by being here. I'm going back, EJ. I won't let him win."

"I'll put Freddie back on your detail."

"I don't want to feel like a prisoner, EJ."

"It's about your safety."

She sighed. "No arguing tonight."

"I agree."

"Do you remember we tried to sneak out to the movies, and you got me grounded?"

I chuckled. "Pretty sure your mom hated that I had you skipping school."

Cora laughed. "Yeah, she did."

"I remember we had sex once at my parents' when they were out. And I remember how jealous I was when you went to college."

"Whenever I told you about a party on campus, you drove up with your brothers to intimidate the boys."

"Well, we're past that time now."

Cora sighed happily. "Still can't believe how lucky I am to have you."

"That goes double for me, baby." I pause. "Lucky enough that I don't have to go to the baby shower?"

"No, sir. You will escort me to the shower." Cora laid her plate on the tray and leaned in to kiss me.

I ran a hand along her back, returning her kiss, the movie forgotten. "I want you to take a break."

"With you?"

I grimaced. "No, I have to work. I was thinking you could go somewhere with your friends. You need to relax."

"Anywhere?"

"The jet is at your disposal."

Chapter 15

Cora

A week later, I was still shaken up by what had happened with Izan and Enrique at the clinic. I poured myself into work and spent time with my friends and EJ's nephews and nieces. Children gave off good energy and kept my mind away from the memory of Izan's body. The news reports about the murder went on for a week, and business at the clinic slowed down as a result, but I decided not to let it get me down.

Deciding to spend time with my friends, I called them up to get some lunch at our favorite lounge.

"Did you see this?" Anissa held a newspaper with a picture of Savio and Vincenzo on the front cover.

"They're opening a casino," I said, glancing at the paper.

Anissa poured the bottle of sparkling water into her glass as Devi gave her order to the server.

"I'll have a burger and fries." Anissa read off the menu.

Devi gulped her Pepsi. "The baby shower is this weekend, and nothing fits me."

"You look beautiful, Devi," I said. "You're glowing."

"The color scheme is gold and cream," Anissa said, sipping her water.

"We have games planned and food you'll love," I added.

"I'm happy you two are planning this for me," Devi said gratefully. She turned to me with a concerned look. "How are you doing after everything, Cora?"

"Honestly, I feel like I'm waiting for the other shoe to drop," I said as the server arrived with our food.

Devi bit into a fry. "What does EJ say?"

"He wants me to move in with him and quit working."

"And be a trophy wife?" Anissa scoffed around a mouthful of burger.

"Probably, but he knows that will never happen." I popped some fires into my mouth. "How is your relationship now?"

"He's the same EJ, but he's more mature. We've both grown up a lot," I said, eating a mouthful of crab cake.

"A baby and ring in a year." Anissa wiggled her finger at me.

"Let's focus on Devi and worry about my love life later." I laughed. "EJ said I can use the private jet for a girls' trip before you have the baby."

Devi leaned in her chair and rubbed her stomach. "I have to check with Wale, but I'm on board for anything by the beach."

I sighed. "Some exotic beach."

"That would be fun," Anissa said excitedly. "I'm so ready to get out of the city."

"Check with your doctor, and I'll find a place for us to go," I told Devi.

"To a girls' trip!" Anissa lifted her glass for a toast.

*** * ***

Saturday came, and I stood in front of the mirror at EJ's, finishing up my makeup for the baby shower. I combed through my full curls, popped in my earrings, and fastened my gold bracelet around my wrist. My high-waisted gold and cream short set was the perfect blend of casual and formal.

Anissa was meeting me at the venue to take care of any last-minute details. Devi had texted me after our lunch two days ago to tell me that Wale was cool with her going on a trip with Anissa and me. I even asked EJ if Mckayla, Rena, and Sonya would like to go with us.

I went to the living room and found EJ on the phone.

"Four on every corner," he said as I slipped on my shoes.

He was already dressed to go and continued to talk on his phone as we left the house. Three cars were lined up behind outside. We would ride in the middle so we were protected front and rear.

Freddie nodded as we slid into the back seat and high-tailed it over the bridge and into the city. EJ finally finished his call and looked me over appreciatively from the tips of my shoes to the top of my head.

Quirked a brow. "Was that about Vargas?"

"I'm ensuring we have enough security."

"I saw the photo of your brothers opening a casino in the paper."

"A few people are trying to halt it."

"Be careful." I reached out to fix his shirt collar.

We reached our destination, and Freddie came around to help me out. EJ captured my hand as we approached the building and opened the door for me to enter first. I spotted large gold and cream balloons hanging on the walls. Giant teddy bears were placed at either end of the table where Devi and Wale would be sitting. A DJ booth was in the corner, and more tables decorated with flowers and baby gifts were spaced at intervals.

"I can't stay the entire time," EJ reminded me.

Anissa and Mitchel appeared holding large gift bags.

"How is the food looking?" I asked as she reached me.

"All set, and the cake is massive," Anissa replied, putting the bags on a nearby gift table.

Devi arrived with Wale, and I left Anissa to get them settled while I spoke to the planner to ensure everything was running smoothly. The DJ started the music just as Mckayla and Rena walked in.

"You two look beautiful," I said as I greeted them.

"You look gorgeous as usual, Cora," Mckayla replied as both women hugged me.

I waved toward a table. "Take a seat. We're about to get started with the first game."

I glanced at Devi to see her talking with Anissa when gunfire pierced the air.

Screams erupted around me, and I watched as Wale yanked Devi to the floor. I scanned the room for EJ and spotted him, gun out as he and his guards ran out of the building and started shooting. His suit and tie were a façade. EJ was deadly when crossed.

The DJ helped some of the women to behind the bar area.

"Cora!" Anissa shouted, urging me toward her, where they were crouched out of sight. Mitchel, Devi, and Wade were with her. I carefully made my way over to them, and we waited for the shooting to stop. The room was full of terrified cries and panicked people calling the police.

The door opened, and EJ came back in with his brothers. His eyes homed in on me. "Cora, are you all right?"

I made a beeline for him, wrapping my arms around his neck. "Was that Enrique?"

"Yeah, and some of his soldiers. We need to clear the place out and get you somewhere safe."

Devi rushed toward us, her face pale. "I need to get to the doctor."

EJ sprang into action. "I'll have one of my men take you to the hospital so they can check you out and ensure you and the baby are okay."

Devi was whisked off. I felt awful. This was all my fault. EJ reached for my hand, but I jerked away.

"I need a minute." I headed for the bathroom and splashed cold water on my face.

Anissa and Rena came in behind me.

"We wanted to check on you." Rena came to stand beside me.

I bit my lip. "If something happens to Devi..."

"You can't think like that. She'll be fine," Rena soothed.

"Am I crazy for doing this again with him?"

"No. Come with me to the house," Rena suggested.

"I'm constantly surrounded by him."

"That's love, Cora," she stressed.

I jumped as the door opened, and EJ entered.

"Renato is waiting for you, Rena," EJ said, gathering me into his arms.

He kissed my forehead, and the four of us left the building to a barrage of police. EJ helped me into the waiting car and turned to speak briefly to Renato and Sante before climbing in beside me.

"Hey, we're fine," he said, reaching for my hand.

"When will he stop?" Enrique's soldiers had attacked without remorse, uncaring about who could have been killed.

"He's a boy sending other people to take care of his business."

I caressed his scarred knuckles. "Where are we going? I want to go check on Devi."

"To my parents' house."

"EJ, she's my best friend."

"Once things calm down, we can visit her."

"Things never seem to calm down with you." Reasoning with EJ was like trying to reason with a brick wall.

We arrived at his parent's house, and I quickly exited the car, pulling out my phone to call for a car service. The phone was snatched out of my hand.

"Give me my phone back," I snarled at EJ.

He wrapped his hand around my throat and crushed his lips to mine.

I bit his bottom lip and pulled away. "Leave me alone."

"Cora, I apologized for today," he said, frustrated.

"Your business is hurting my friends," I hissed, jerking out of his grip.

"Come inside so we can talk."

"I'm going home."

"No, you're not."

"Yes. I. Am." I marched up to the car. "Freddie, drive me home, or so help me God, I will walk."

Freddie glanced at EJ, who gave him a slight nod.

I needed space to wrap my head around what had happened and to decide if I could live this life.

* * *

As soon as I got back to my apartment, I texted Devi.

Me: *Are you okay?*

Devi: *I'm fine. So is the baby.*

Me: *Thank God. Call me when you can.*

I opened a bottle of wine and ran myself a bath, relaxing in the hot water for a long time. Once I was done, I grabbed leftover cake from the fridge and settled on the couch.

I jumped up at the knock at my front door. I selfishly hoped it was EJ, but I was surprised to see my mother.

"How did you get here?"

She slipped off her jacket and placed it on the loveseat with her purse. "I had the butler drop me off."

"Are you hungry?"

"No. I wanted to check on you."

"I'm waiting for Devi to call me back. I texted her earlier. She and the baby are fine," I said, sitting on the couch.

Mom dropped down beside me. "Hopefully, they'll be home soon."

"You didn't have to come all this way."

"Of course I did. You're my daughter. I was on my way to the event and heard what happened."

"Oh, geez. I forgot about you and Adelina." I reached for the landline.

"She's okay. EJ told her you were here and needed space."

"Adelina's always been good to me."

"EJ's worried about you."

"Sometimes, I feel like our love is a fairy tale, and other times, it seems like a nightmare because of his family's mob life."

"He loves you more than anyone, Cora." She stroked my hair as I lay my head on her lap. "I was young once. Love is tricky."

My head snapped up as the front door opened, and EJ entered. I avoided his gaze as he headed straight for my bedroom.

"Talk to him," Mom said.

"He wants me to leave my apartment and job."

"Do what makes you happy, Cora."

"Thank you." I climbed off the couch and sauntered. Standing in the doorway, I watched as he removed his jacket and kicked off his shoes. "You have a house."

"I like this place better."

"We can't keep going back and forth, EJ. I'm tired of being a walking target."

He sat on the edge of the bed and stretched out a hand. I moved toward him, and he pulled me onto his lap. "I'm sorry you're in the middle of all this."

"Maybe it's time to get out of the business."

"Cora, I can't do that."

"You want me to leave my life, but you can't do the same thing." I yanked away.

"It's not that simple. This is my family's life."

"What about *my* life?"

We glared at each other. This conversation was getting us nowhere and putting us both in a bad mood. I just wanted to sleep and forget what had happened today.

Mom had gone when I returned to the living room, no doubt making herself scarce while we talked. I lay on the couch with a blanket and watched movies until I fell asleep. Sometime in the middle of the night, EJ woke me carrying me back to the bedroom.

"Sorry for falling asleep," I murmured.

"Make it up to me."

I turned to face him in bed, running a hand down his chest and inside his boxers to grip his heavy rod. "How would you like me to do that, Mr. Calabresi?"

EJ's jaw was covered in a light scruff where he hadn't shaved. I took in his full lips, chiseled jawline, and thick lashes. I loved that mouth of his, how he swirled his long tongue across my clit and sucked on my nipples. Perfect. I wanted to ride him all night.

He moaned as I leaned in and sucked on his neck. "Stop teasing me, Cora."

I grinned wickedly. "I like teasing you."

I pushed him onto his back, and he gripped my thighs as I straddled his hips. I bent, kissing him deeply, our tongues sliding together.

EJ whispered, "You are my love. My everything, Cora."

Chapter 16

Elio Jr

A war started two weeks after the shootout at the baby shower. Both families showed no mercy in touching each other's businesses. I got approval from Savio to steal shipments of their cocaine in Mexico. Enrique and Cacho retaliated by robbing a few of our warehouses. The Vargas Cartel had expanded into more of our territory, selling their drugs and stealing our guns.

Sante managed to get the word around town to our suppliers not to do business with the Vargas Cartel. We worked late nights to ensure our soldiers were on top of what needed to happen and when to strike. We needed to make a statement that we weren't backing down from this fight.

My father received a call from the governor about how we were making too much noise in Chicago, so Savio and I went to meet with him. We sat in his office, waiting for him to arrive. He finally walked in with a few of his lackeys as if they could intimate us.

"Savio. EJ." Governor Roy tipped his head at us and sank into his chair.

I nodded. "Governor Roy."

The governor lifted a cigar from a box on his desk. "I'm not very happy with what I'm seeing."

Savio narrowed his eyes. "We agree."

I looked from my brother to Governor Roy, waiting for him to reassure my brother that he was still on board with the casino.

"What are you planning on doing to fix the situation?" Governor Roy questioned.

"The situation is more complicated than we anticipated."

Governor Roy pounded his fist on the desk. "I know, based on the phone calls and news channel reports from all the bodies piling up in the morgue!"

My brow spiked at his aggression. "Governor Roy, I suggest you watch your tone when you talk to us.

He tensed and looked at his bodyguard. "The city is on fire because of you and your wars. One of you needs to stand down."

Something about his tone and suggestion were off.

"What did he promise you?"

Governor Roy frowned. "Who?"

"You can only pretend for so long, Governor. I seem to recall that my family donated the highest amount to your election campaign," I reminded him.

The governor gulped water from the glass on his desk and coughed nervously. I opened my briefcase, removed a yellow envelope, and tossed it onto his desk. He reached for it hesitantly, and his face turned red as he removed the contents.

"Those are photos of you meeting with Cacho Vargas, correct?"

"Where did you get these?" the governor spluttered.

"We have eyes everywhere, Roy. We know about your little gambling problem and your debts with the Vargas Cartel."

Governor Roy rubbed the back of his neck. "That's none of your business."

"Keep looking, Roy."

The last two photos showed him snorting cocaine with a woman who wasn't his wife. Vincenzo had pulled more evidence, but I suspected the governor would fold easily with these four pictures. I still had a few more aces up my sleeve—the illegitimate child in another state that he wasn't paying support for and proof he was stealing from his wife's account to pay off his mistresses. Roy wouldn't last long if I learned he was playing both sides.

"How do I know you didn't fake these photos?"

I leaned forward so he could hear me. Savio gripped my arm to stop me from getting in his face. "The only reason you're in this position is because of me. The board voted to dismiss you, but I convinced them to give you another chance."

"Listen, I can do the job, but you're putting me in a bad situation with a few higher-ups," Roy argued, the veins popping in his forehead.

"The only people you answer to are us."

"Here's the deal, Governor. You cut all ties with the Vargas Cartel, or you'll be looking for another job," Savio informed him.

Savio and I rose from our chairs.

"Keep the photos. We have plenty more," I said as a parting shot.

Savio stopped me outside of the building. "You looked ready to kill him."

"He's playing us, Savio."

Savio's forehead creased as he frowned. "Roy knows we can handle him. What's really pissing you off?"

Savio had always been like a second father to us growing up, someone we could go to for advice and help, especially if we fucked up.

I flexed my jaw. "I'm trying to keep Cora safe, and she's fighting me at every turn."

Savio shoved his hands in his pockets. "You know, I went through the same thing with Mckayla."

"She's not the same as Cora."

"And that's a bad thing?"

"I don't know." I was wound up and suspicious of every person who came in my direction. Being with Cora gave me peace, but I could admit I became a little neglectful when I lost myself in work.

We climbed into the car and fastened our seatbelts. My thoughts were jammed together, and I was worried about how we could ensure the Governor stayed under our control.

"Play it safe and triple up on her security or make her live with you," Savio said.

I shook my head. "She's not Mckayla."

"Don't give her a choice. We heard from our sources that Cacho is talking about leaving for Mexico."

"He can try, but the only way he'll leave is in a body bag."

"I'll pay the governor another visit in a few weeks. For now, give him a little time to get his mind right," Savio recommended.

I thought about it for a few seconds before nodding. Savio's phone rang, and as he answered, mine vibrated in my pocket.

Cora: *You left early this morning.*

Me: *Business meeting.*

Cora: *Are you at the office?*

Me: *On the way back now.*

Cora: *I'm here with lunch.*

Me: *You should have told me you wanted to have lunch together.*

Cora: *It's my surprise.*

Me: *See you in five minutes.*

Cora: *See you soon.*

* * *

My assistant handed me the files ready for me to sign and told me Cora was waiting in my office. I shut the door behind me and tossed the documents on my desk. Cora was sitting on the couch, and I lifted her onto my lap.

She cupped my chin and kissed me on the lips. "How was the meeting?"

I ran my hand along her thigh. "Like any other meeting. I had to put my foot down."

Cora picked up the baked potatoes and steaks. "What do you think about dinner tonight?"

"Where?"

"My place."

"You're going to cook for me?"

Cora lifted the fork to my mouth and fed me some of the steak. "I told my friends about the vacation you're treating me to, and I wanted to show you how much I appreciate you being patient."

"We've navigated some crazy waters together, huh?"

"We sure have. And my mom loves you." Cora rolled her eyes at her statement.

I grinned. "Marilyn brought you to me."

"I feel the same way."

"What time are you thinking for dinner?"

"Probably seven or eight. I have some paperwork to finish up at the office." Cora sprinkled some salt over her food.

"You didn't drive here today, did you?"

"No, but I plan on driving myself to work," she said, wiping her mouth with the napkin.

"We've talked about this, Cora. It's not safe right now."

"The guards can follow me."

"Not enough. I need eyes on you at all times."

"We're not discussing this right now."

We vetted new soldiers every day to work for the family. If Cora thought she would win this battle, she was mistaken.

"Come on, feed me, and tell me what you plan on doing for your trip." I gently tapped her ass.

"Maybe Atlantic City."

"I thought you wanted to go to the beach? Devi's had the baby now."

"Exactly, and Wale doesn't want her to leave at all, but she needs a break for a minute to relax."

I fiddled with the charm bracelet her mom bought her for her thirteenth birthday. "Atlantic City isn't far. You can be back in a few days."

Cora pressed her lips to mine. "Yep, so can you book the dates for me."

I pulled out my cell phone. "I'll have my assistant call the pilot to prepare the jet for you."

"Give me a week or two."

"All right. Just remember, you have a man who will burn the city down if harm comes to you."

Cora placed the food on the table and gazed into my eyes.

I cupped the back of her neck, and the softness of her skin sent chills down my spine. "You're sexy today."

Cora looked down at herself. "It's just a skirt and a shirt."

I ran my fingers down her throat. "Not to me."

"What are you doing?" she whispered.

I slowly leaned in and brushed a kiss along her jawline. "Tasting what's mine."

"We can't."

"Why not? It's my office."

"People will hear." She glanced at the window where the blinds were closed and bit her lip.

My dick strained in my pants. "I'm not the only one ready to fuck. I can smell your arousal."

Cora ran a hand down my chest as she moved against me. "Temptress."

"Only for you."

I sighed, forcing my body to calm. "Much as I hate to break up our lunch date, I do have to finish some work."

She nodded and rose from my lap. "Call me when you're on the way to my place."

I stopped her as she started to clean up. "Don't worry about the trash. I'll get it later." I walk her toward the door and pull it open. "Have a good afternoon."

I kissed her, sliding my tongue into her mouth. Gripping her ass, I pressed her against my erection. Before I changed my mind, I released her, and she wiped her lipstick from my lips.

"See you later," she murmured.

"Call me when you make it home."

"I will."

* * *

Hours later, I closed my computer, weary from long phone calls and meetings with the board. I filed the final documents for the casino property and stood, picking up my keys and jacket and locking the office door behind me. My assistant wrapped up her phone call and took the files I handed her.

"Those need to be sent to Vincenzo to be read over."

"Of course, Mr. Calabresi."

I checked the time on my watch. "Take off for the day."

"I need to get a few more things on your calendar."

"It can wait for tomorrow."

She smiled and thanked me.

I headed to the elevator as someone stepped out and hopped on, pressing the button for the main lobby. I met Freddie at the front of the building and slipped into the back seat. Tossing my jacket beside me, I pulled out my phone and smiled as I scrolled through some old photos of Cora and me.

"Where to, Boss?"

"Cora's."

"Heads up," Freddie said.

I looked behind me and noticed a black vehicle riding two cars behind us. "Drive around to make sure we're not being tailed."

My phone rang, and I answered.

"We may have a problem," Roy muttered.

"Problem, Governor?"

"He's not letting me cut ties with him."

"That's not my problem."

"Listen to me, Elio. What you want will worsen things for everybody."

"Governor, we talked about what you need to do, or Enrique Vargas won't be your only problem."

"He's saying I have to pay, and I don't have the money."

"Your debt is on you. Your family is at home?"

"What?"

"Your wife and child are home right now, and you're at the office, correct?"

"Wait a minute."

"I have trained shooters around your mansion and staff inside who will take them out with one phone call from me."

Governor Roy pleaded, "Please! We can come up with a better plan."

"Then figure it out."

"Enrique wants me to deny the casino land to your family."

My spine stiffened. I closed my eyes to control my temper, gripping my gun. "We break ground in a few months. Do you really want to piss me off, Roy?" I pounded my fist against the car seat.

"Maybe if you're able to pay a little more," he suggested.

I chuckled. "You're a piece of work."

"I got in over my head and needed more to pay for some things for my wife."

"Blackmailing my family to pay off your debts does not look good for you, Roy."

"A million is nothing to you."

"Get off my phone and find a better habit to manage besides drugs. I'd hate to see you wash up from the lake." I ended the call.

Freddie turned off the freeway, and I noticed the other vehicle was gone. Relief washed over me. As we pulled up at Cora's apartment building, I instructed him to keep an eye on the area and call me if anything came up.

A delicious aroma teased my nostrils as I let myself into the apartment. Cora was in the kitchen on the phone. I shut the door behind me, dropped my stuff on the couch, and went to wash up and change before dinner.

Grabbing t-shirts and lounge pants, I entered the bathroom to shower the day away.

"Hi." Cora stood at the door.

"You want to join me?" I turned the water hotter.

"No. We won't get to dinner if that happens." She giggled and turned to walk away.

"Dinner's overrated!" I yelled, hopping into the shower.

We spent the night laughing and talking about Cora's plans for the girls' trip. She was even thinking about taking Mom along to get away. Later, we lay in bed, watching movies and eating popcorn until we fell asleep.

Chapter 17

Cora

Mckayla set a tray of chips, dips, and fruit on the table. I leaned over to dip a chip in the onion dip and popped it into my mouth. Gulping the strawberry stella rosa, I listened to Sonya tell a story about EJ getting into trouble with his father.

All the girls had come to Mckayla's today for lunch. Savio had expanded the backyard for the kids and added an area for Mckayla to hang out with family and friends.

EJ left my place before breakfast, and I met up with Julia and Colson to make sure they were still on board with working at the clinic after the shootout.

Rena topped up her glass and sat next to me on the balcony.

"This is good, Mckayla," I said, tucking into the chips and salsa.

"How are things with you and EJ?" she asked.

"He's good. We're good." EJ and I were like an old married couple, talking about our day and work. He smiled and joked like the old EJ, and my fears about our future were gradually melting away. I'd decided not to listen to the bad parts of his work, and we'd set boundaries to ensure neither of us neglected the other.

"All the news channels reported the shooting. Did they catch them?" Sonya asked.

"No clue. I let EJ handle it."

Rena topped up her glass and sat next to me on the balcony. "They hate it when we try to get involved in their business."

Sonya poured more dressing on her salad. "Yep. I learned that quickly. Devi, how is the baby doing?"

Devi sipped her water. "She's amazing. Sleeping through the night." She passed her phone around the table, showing pictures of her baby girl.

Warmth filled my chest seeing their child. "She looks just like Wale."

"Please don't tell him that. His ego is already huge," Devi joked.

"How about we go out tonight?" Rena suggested. "Being wives and mothers doesn't mean our lives are over."

"Where would we go?" Anissa asked.

Rena shrugged. "To a club or something."

"It would be hard to find a babysitter at short notice," Mckayla said.

"I'm sure Adelina would watch them," Rena replied.

I grimaced. "EJ might get pissed."

"Why?" Rena probed.

"He's on edge because of the Vargas situation."

"We all have protection," Sonya said. "We need a girl's night out."

"I'll pass. Wale is still pissed about the shooting," Devi replied.

"I'm sorry about what happened," I said for the hundredth time.

Devi covered my palm with hers. "Nothing to apologize for. It's not your fault you're in the middle of a mafia war. It'll do us good to get away for a few days."

"Where are you going?" Sonya asked, passing a piece of fruit to RJ.

"Atlantic City. It's close, so Devi won't be too far away if she needs to get back for the baby. "If you guys want to come, we have EJ's private jet for the trip."

Rena clinked glasses with me. "That sounds good. A girl's weekend."

"Away from Savio and the boys." Mckayla clapped her hands in excitement.

"Private jet, food, gambling, and dancing." I snapped my fingers, dancing in my seat.

"What else is going on with you?" Mckayla asked, rising from her seat and collecting up the trash. She wore a two-piece bikini showing off her sexy figure after having another baby.

"Remember I told you about how Enrique tried to use me to get to EJ?"

Everybody nodded, waiting for me to continue.

"His brother bumped into me in New York, and I had no idea."

Rena frowned. "Wait, so they were spying on you?"

"That's what EJ told me. I was shocked because he's the one who tried to buy me out of the clinic."

Mckayla whistled. "Crazy how dirty they get."

Anissa shook her head. "He's the one who was killed."

"I hate having a blood bath surrounding me, but murder is part of the life they lead. At first, I thought EJ was trying to control my life because he was jealous, but now I know differently."

Silence fell for a minute before Rena started talking about going to a club and how we should all dress sexy. I smiled as I watched the kids roaming around the back-yard, playing with their toys and jumping in the pool.

Mckayla gasped at SJ trying to dive into the water without his nanny. "He's stubborn, like his father," she said, jumping up and rushing toward the pool.

* * *

I finished applying my mascara, fluffing up my lashes. I'd used a soft nude color palette on my face. Smiling, I checked my teeth to ensure there was no lipstick staining them. I wore a long red dress that dipped to expose the length of my back while keeping my front covered. Pleased with how I looked, I spritzed myself with my favorite Fenty beauty perfume.

Music blasted in my apartment. Anissa had grabbed her clothes and come back to my place to get ready so we could ride together. Devi told me she'd message if she could come and hang with us for a few hours while the baby slept.

"How do I look?" Anisa turned in front of me.

"Mitchel let you out of the house with that dress?" I teased, taking in the low-cut strapless leather dress.

"He doesn't know." Anissa winked at me.

"Grab the black animal print heels from my closet. They'll go perfectly with that dress."

"Hair up or down?"

"Down."

Anissa fixed her hair and grinned at me. "Are you ready?"

"Ready." I checked my phone to see a message from Devi.

Devi: *I'll meet you there.*

Me: *Great! Tell Wale we said thank you.*

Devi: *I owe him a few blow jobs.*

Me: *Well, I'll leave that to you.*

I laughed and closed out of the thread, grabbing a shawl for my shoulders and turning out the bedroom lights.

"Is she coming?" Anissa asked.

"Yep. She said Wale told her she had to pay in blowjobs."

"Men." Anissa giggled.

"Let's go so we can meet them on time."

"It's been so long since we had a night out." Anissa walked in front of me, and I shut the door.

"Jason, you remember Anissa." I reintroduced my bodyguard to Anissa for the night. He stuck his hand out for a shake and held the elevator door for us.

"Dancing and drinking, here we come." Anissa twisted her hips and snapped her fingers excitedly as we sauntered to the car.

James checked the surrounding area and opened the car door. Being on alert was second nature now, but I refused to let Enrique's actions control my life. James whipped the escalade out of the parking structure and into the traffic, speeding up to pass the yellow light.

"We have VIP tonight, right?" Anissa asked.

"Rena more than likely has VIP if Renato owns the place."

"I'm glad we can do things like this together." Anissa held up her phone and stuck out her tongue to take a selfie. "Smile."

The smooth sounds of Doja Cat played in the car. James parked out front of the club, cut the engine, and helped us out before escorting us through the private entrance.

"We'll call you when we're ready," I told him.

He nodded and waited outside. I noticed Rena standing with the girls in the booth and waved to get her attention. She tapped her guard on the shoulder to come to get us, and I thanked him when he helped us through the crowd. Anissa went for the bottles first while I hugged everyone and said hello.

"Renato bought this place, right?" I asked.

Sonya nodded. "Last month. He wanted to test it out first to see how busy it was and liked how it vibed." She grabbed a glass of champagne and passed it to me, clinking it with hers in a toast.

"Oooh, we're getting crashed, ladies," Anissa said, looking behind me.

I turned to see EJ, Vincenzo, and Renato stalking through the crowd as women tried to get their attention. EJ paused to talk to one of the guards before sitting beside me.

"Are you stalking me, sir?" I cocked my head to the side.

"I have business here. Renato and Vincenzo tagged along."

"Why don't I believe you?"

He smirked as he picked up my hand and kissed my knuckles. "You can trust me, baby."

EJ pulled me out off the couch and wrapped his

hands around my waist, burying his head in my neck. "How long have you been here?" he asked over the music.

"A few minutes."

"Are you coming home with me?"

"If that's what you want?"

"It's what I want." He lifted my chin and stared into my eyes.

I smiled and kissed him. "Go handle business."

A movement over his shoulder caught my eyes, and I tensed as I saw Enrique standing near the entrance with another man. "Oh, fuck."

"What?" EJ pulled back and followed my line of sight.

"Nothing."

"Cora? Is something wrong?"

"No. I thought I saw something, but my mind is playing tricks on me."

A figment of my imagination. There was no way Enrique followed us here without James noticing him. I wanted to enjoy my night without any problems like an average person my age, not dodging bullets.

I raised my glass and took another sip. "Go handle your work. I have plans to hit the dance floor."

"Make sure no one dances with you."

"What's the fun in dancing alone?" I pouted.

"Anissa and Rena can dance with you," EJ replied.

Devi popped up behind him, and I extended my arms to hug her. "You made it!"

"Little one finally calmed down so I could leave," Devi responded.

I led her to the table, and she sat next to Mckayla. "EJ, you remember Devi."

EJ nodded and said hello. "Be good." He tapped me on the butt.

Anissa pulled me away and led me to the dancefloor with guards surrounding us to keep the men away. I was embarrassed but welcomed having fun with the girls, even with our guys showing up.

The DJ changed the flow to Arianna Grande. The crowd went wild, and the party really got started. Anissa and I pretended to sing the song to each other in a competition, and it was the most fun. As I whirled and threw my hands in the air, someone bumped into me, knocking me to the ground.

"Hey, watch where you're going!" Anissa yelled to the girl who'd bumped me. She reached out to help me up, and I wiped off my dress.

The girl glared at me coldly before walking toward the back exit. She leaned into a man and whispered in his ear. I couldn't see his face because of the crowd, but tension seized me as I wondered if Enrique was here tonight.

Anissa booty bumped me." Hey, what's the matter?"

"Huh?"

"Do you know her?"

"Uh, no. Come on, let's go. I'm tired."

"We just got down here."

"I know, but my feet are killing me."

We headed back to our section, and I listened to the girls talk about their upcoming plans and the girls' trip. EJ returned to our section an hour and a half later, and I left the girls to go home with him.

* * *

"You seem distracted," EJ said, removing his cufflinks.

I slipped off my shoes. "I'm fine."

"Anissa said someone bumped into you."

"It was nothing."

EJ's expression showed he didn't believe me. I pulled his shirt from his pants and slowly unbuttoned it. Leaning forward, I pressed a kiss on his chest.

"Cora, hold up."

"No, you're always doing it for me. Tonight is about you."

His hand came around the back of my neck, pulling me away. "Are you trying to keep me from questioning you?"

"I'm fine, babe. You worry too much. Relax for me." I took him by the hand and led him to the bathroom.

Turning on the shower, I undressed him and slid my dress off. He watched me pin my hair in a tight bun before opening the shower door. I stepped inside and let the water cascade over my face. EJ came in behind me, and I climbed on his lap as he sat on the bench seat.

"When you touch me, I sometimes think I'm not worthy of your love," he confessed.

"Is that your fear?" I whispered, gripping his large girth and easing down on him. We both moaned in ecstasy.

"My fear is not being able to keep you forever."

I moved my hips back and forth slowly. He had no idea how much I needed and wanted him more every day. He gripped my hips as I moved on him, and I bent to bite his shoulder to keep from screaming.

His deep eyes burned with desire, and I pushed a finger into his mouth, bouncing faster and faster in his lap.

"Ugh, EJ," I moaned, removing my finger.

EJ stuck his thumb in my mouth before sliding it into my ass, pumping his hips harder and faster. I began to shake, digging my nails into his shoulders as my orgasm hit me. EJ grunted as he released his seed inside me, falling into my chest and sucking my nipples.

"We forgot to shower." I giggled.

He surged to his feet with me in his arms, pushed me against the wall, and fucked me again.

Chapter 18

Elio Jr

The weekend arrived, and I had to go to a stupid business event without Cora because she had to work last minute. Governor Roy was still trying to dodge us, but we decided to take him up on the charity fundraising event his wife was putting on. The exposure of a charity event would be good for the family name. Savio, Vincenzo, and Renato joined me to make sure Roy knew we meant business about him cutting ties with the Vargas Cartel.

Roy's wife, Constantine, had decided to hold the event at the governor's mansion. A piano played in the back room, and the tables were decorated with the finest china and gold-plated nameplates. Security surrounded the entire grounds, protecting close to sixty people tonight.

I placed my empty glass on the bar and motioned to the bartender for another shot. I scanned the crowd of prissy snobs laughing and talking about which of their many houses they would vacation in for the summer.

Most people here took money from people like me to keep up appearances and fake their importance in the press.

Renato bumped my arm. "He's on his way over."

I gulped the rest of my drink and asked for another.

Governor Roy held his wife's hand. "Gentleman, I didn't expect you all to show up."

"We wouldn't miss your wife's event, Governor." I smiled.

"Hello, I'm Constantine," his wife introduced herself, extending her hand.

Savio shook it, but I kissed her knuckles. "Good thing your husband kept you away from us. You are beautiful, Mrs. Hudson."

Constantine's eyes gleamed at my compliment. "How do you gentlemen know my husband?"

"We do business together. Your husband is why our casino is coming to Chicago," I taunted.

The governor choked on his drink, and Constantine patted his back.

"Drink went down the wrong way, Governor?" Renato joked.

Roy's eye twitched nervously, and he loosened his tie. "I have to talk with them for a second, my love. Give me a moment." The governor nudged her to go with security.

"You look a little flustered, Roy," I remarked.

The governor took a step toward me, but Vincenzo pushed him back. "Please tell me you're not here to ruin my wife's charity event!" he spat.

"Give us the five million you owe."

"I don't have it."

"Then shut the fuck up, do as I say, and cut ties with the Vargas Cartel before he gets you killed."

"He's trying to buy the land you plan to use for the casino."

I laughed and picked up the butter knife from the bar top. I moved close and pressed the knife to his side. "The casino is bought and paid for, and everything included is owned by Calabresi Holdings. I think it's time we have a little talk alone, Governor."

"Stay calm, and no one will get hurt," Renato said, lifting his jacket to reveal his gun.

The governor's guards scanned the scene. I smiled like everything was normal, but they started to move closer.

I clenched my teeth. "Tell them you're fine."

"Governor, is there a problem?" one of his guards asked, checking us over.

"The governor has had too much to drink. Ain't that right, Roy?"

Roy hesitated, and I cleared my throat. "Yeah, my wife's going to kill me for drinking the rum she ordered for guests." He laughed, and we joined in on the joke.

"Looks like they're about to begin the bidding," Vincenzo said.

"Ladies and gentlemen." Constantine waved at the crowd from the stage.

"Guys, I'm going to my office for a moment. I'll be right back," Roy told his guards. They started to follow, and the governor stopped them. "Keep an eye on my wife. My office is only around the corner."

"We'll be right here, sir," his guard replied.

* * *

I slammed the governor's face into the desk, gripping his hair as blood spilled from his nose. "Do you want to die, Roy? Huh? Answer me, goddamn it!"

"I'm sorry."

"The time for apologies is gone. We're done playing nice with you," I said.

"Take him out of the back hallway and get him in the car to the warehouse," Savio instructed.

Roy shuddered. "Hold up! You...you can't kill me."

"I can do anything I want," Savio said coldly.

"What about our deal?" Roy strained his neck, his eyes popping wide.

"Our deal ended the minute your drug and gambling problem overshadowed our business. My father taught us to have a backup plan," I informed him.

The door opened, and Constantine walked inside with a stern look.

Roy glanced from Constantine to me.

"What is going on in here? And don't give me excuses, Roy. I tried to help you years ago," Constantine spat.

"I can change, I promise," Roy begged. "It's not that bad."

"Not bad? Look at yourself," Constantine snapped.

"I borrowed the money for you," Roy whined.

Constantine marched around the desk and cuffed him under the chin. "A widow is better for an election campaign, anyway. I'll tell our children you loved them." She released him, walked around the desk, and left the room.

"Constantine! You can't leave me here!" Roy screamed.

Renato slipped on his black gloves, removed his gun, and shot Roy in the head.

"Make it look like a suicide," I said, scanning his desk.

Vincenzo went through his cabinets and found drugs.

"Get rid of the guards." I left the room and returned to the party like nothing had happened. Grabbing a drink from the bar, I stepped close to the stage as Constantine made another auction announcement and raised my glass in acknowledgment. I mingled with a few politicians until Renato and Vincenzo returned, confirming that the cleanup was done.

"Thank you again for the invitation, Mrs. Hudson. I hope you hit your target tonight."

"Thank you for coming, and I'll let my husband know about your generous donation," Constantine answered.

Renato talked on his phone as we left the mansion, leaving the sudden gasps of shock and screams behind. It seemed someone had found Roy.

"The sirens must be coming," Renato said, ending his call.

Vincenzo lifted his chin. "Check that out."

I looked in the direction he indicated and saw Cacho talking with a woman. That meant Enrique was close by, but we couldn't take him out after killing the governor.

I grabbed Renato's hand as he went for his gun. "Too busy."

Renato paused. "We can take two out in one night."

"Not the time," I responded.

"He's right, Renato," Vincenzo agreed.

"We need to head home and regroup. Reporters will be all over this place asking questions tomorrow."

Renato put his gun away. "I'll let it slide. For now."

* * *

The entire board sat around the conference room and watched the developments happen in real-time. The death of the Governor, the scandal of him having drugs on him, and gambling debts amounting to millions of dollars.

Savio switched to another channel.

"Reports are still coming in on the sudden death of Governor Roy Hudson," a news reporter explained.

Vincenzo turned to face us from the front of the room. "While this news is upsetting, we have to think about the future of our casino and the expanding hotel."

"Should we keep the property or move in a different direction?" Alexander, a board member who started with my father, asked.

"Our deal is solidified, and a silent partner has already signed off the property," Vincenzo answered.

"Who's the partner? Roy is dead," he questioned.

"His wife," I replied.

The room erupted in chatter, and Savio raised his hand for them to be quiet. "Vincenzo will move forward and start construction soon. We're moving into breaking ground. Roy mishandled funds, but that has nothing to do with us."

"Calabresi Holding ties will look suspicious if we don't halt production," Alexander pointed out.

"News reporters can dig up whatever they want. Our paperwork is legit," I explained.

Vincenzo continued discussing his ideas for the layout of the hotel and the casino grounds and how much the budget was expected to hit.

I sat around after the meeting, listening to Savio talk

with the police in his office. Attending the charity event last night put our family firmly in the spotlight.

"So, you said he was alive when you left the party?" one of the detectives inquired.

"He was," Savio confirmed.

"What about you? Did you see or hear anything?" he asked, looking at me.

I leaned back in my chair. "He was laughing and talking with his family."

"How long have you been planning a casino in Chicago?"

"Why is that a question?" I cut in before Savio could answer.

"Just covering all the bases," the other detective remarked.

"A lot of people at the party did business with the Hudson family," Savio pointed out.

"His wife wants to bury him immediately and continue running as his replacement in office," the detective said.

"Good for her. We need more female politicians." I smirked.

The detective pulled a business card from his pocket and placed it on Savio's desk. "If you can think of anything else, please call this number."

"Was it ruled murder?" Savio asked.

"No, but I like to cover every angle," he said as he stood.

Savio and I stared at their backs and waited for the door to close as they left the office.

I stood and turned to face the window. "All bases are covered," I confirmed before Savio could ask.

"I trust you cleaned up properly." Savio rose and strolled to the bar to pour himself a drink.

"Renato wiped all the cameras, and Vincenzo ensured his wife understood her position."

Savio sipped his drink and sighed. "I've taught you well."

I chortled as I glanced at him. "Fuck you."

"When's this girls' trip happening? My wife wants to leave me, and I have you to blame."

"It's a weekend getaway."

"Still too long to be away from her."

"Cora has Mom watching the kids with Marilyn if you need help."

"I can handle my kids."

I chuckled at his statement. "I can't wait to get a call from you about how the kids are driving you crazy."

Savio waved me off as he passed me a glass of cognac. As I raised the glass to my mouth, the door burst open, and Vincenzo exploded inside.

"What?" I asked.

"We might have a problem." Vincenzo marched over and held up a newspaper.

"Tell me?" Savio instructed.

"'Did the Calabresi Cartel have a hand in the death of Governor Hudson.'" I read the headline and tossed the paper on the ground.

"Get the reporter on the phone," Savio demanded.

Vincenzo said, "Don't threaten anyone. We need a relationship with the press."

Picking up the phone, I dialed the owners of the newspapers we'd done business with in the past. The call went to voicemail.

"No one's answering." I listened to the voicemail.

Vincenzo crossed his arms over his chest. "They know."

"Prepare a statement and send it to our publicist," Savio advised.

"Make sure it's direct and factual. 'Calabresi Holdings Inc is saddened about the passing of Roy Hudson and sends our condolences.' Any statements or claims that defame our name will be met with a lawsuit." I spoke to Vincenzo, who wrote down every word to prepare our team to get it out to the public.

"We'll go to the funeral to show our support," Savio added.

I left to return to my office, leaving them to handle the details.

Chapter 19

Cora

Julia flipped the sign to "closed" on the clinic door. I logged out of the receptionist's computer as she picked up the file folders to put away.

"Are we talking about a girls' trip or being with your boyfriend?" Julia teased.

"It's a girls' trip, and EJ paid for everything. He's even letting me use the private jet."

"Go ahead and confess that you like being back in his arms." Julia turned to face me.

I grinned and went to my office to grab my purse and jacket.

EJ had taken me on dates, and we'd made great progress with communication. We'd come a long way from when I ignored him at family gatherings a few months ago. Now, I went to sleep and woke up in his arms.

He'd called me earlier about dealing with the reporters covering the governor's death. Anytime something like this happened, the media tried to make everyone out to be the bad guy.

"Did you see all the news reports about the governor? The press says that EJ and his brothers were at the party?"

"The family goes to a lot of parties and charity events."

"So terrifying. I liked him as governor." Julia stood at the office door as I finished cleaning up.

"Wasn't he in his second term?"

Julia held her hand out to take the trash from me. "He just got re-elected. I can drop the trash off."

"Thanks."

Enrique and Cacho hadn't come by or tried to hurt EJ's business, so I'd assumed the war was over, or a truce had been reached. I fluffed my hair and replaced my heels with my flats, accompanying Julia to the back door.

"So, how are things with you and EJ?" she asked.

"Good. He's different. I can't forget what happened, but I know he cares a lot about me."

"I'm happy for you, Cora. A love like yours shouldn't be destroyed by not overcoming differences."

"I had a lot of grief and anger toward him initially, but now it's been replaced with love."

"So glad he understood about the miscarriage."

'Took a while, especially with him being extra possessive."

"Is that guy still trying to get you to go on a date with him?"

"No, thankfully," I replied, setting the alarm and locking the door behind me.

Julia needed a ride home tonight since her car was in the garage. EJ was working late at the office, so I planned to soak in the tub, eat, and go to bed.

"Oh, I forgot my phone," Julia said as we reached my

car. "I need to run back inside." I started to go with her, but she waved me off. "Stay. It'll only take me a second."

I nodded and passed her the keys to open the door.

"Be right back." Julia hurried to the employee entrance just as an almighty *boom* exploded through the evening.

"Julia!" I screamed, running toward the cloud of fire and smoke. It was too thick, and I started to cough.

"Oh, God!" another voice yelled.

I tried again to run toward the fire.

Boom!

The force of the explosion tossed me back. I hit the ground hard, and everything went dark.

* * *

EJ tried everything to get me to talk to him, but the guilt from Julia's death was eating me up. I was in the hospital for a few days following the explosion, a bomb planted by the Vargas Cartel as payback for Izan's death. I'd told the guys so many times that I didn't need around-the-clock protection, and now I was forced to face the reality of living with Elio Jr. He was the love of my life, a lawyer by day and a mobster by night.

"How long have I been asleep?" I was lying in his bed. When I left the hospital, he'd brought me to his place, along with some of my things.

He leaned against the headboard, caressing my cheek. "A few hours. Food is ready if you're hungry."

"I can't eat right now." I tried to sit up and felt a tightness in my chest. I grimaced and lay back down again.

"Slow down, baby. You're still healing," EJ advised gently.

I captured his hand. I felt like our world was crumbling. "What are we doing?"

"What do you mean?"

"Us. So many people are getting hurt."

EJ silenced me with a kiss. "I'm sorry about your friend." He wiped the tears from my cheek.

"Have you heard from her family?"

"Not yet."

"I feel so much guilt. It's my fault."

"Nothing that's happened is your fault."

"Don't pacify me, EJ. I know what I signed up for when I—" I stopped abruptly.

"When you what?" His brow dipped low.

I sighed and shook my head. "Nothing."

"Are you regretting us?"

I started to cry and tried to move away, covering my face. EJ wrapped me in his arms, and I cried myself to sleep.

* * *

A week rolled by. I stayed at EJ's place, running back and forth to grab what I needed from my apartment. He was still demanding that I move in with him, but I thought it was too soon. The girls' trip was put on hold while I recouped and regained my strength.

"Yes, I want to look at locations whenever you have time," I told the real estate agent EJ used for his properties. I placed the call on speaker, removing the milk and bread from the grocery bag and putting them away.

"I can pick some places out in a few days for us to look at."

"Thank you, Flora."

"You're welcome. I know you wanted a standalone location," Flora said.

Putting the empty bags in the trash, I grabbed eggs and cheese from the fridge to start cooking. "A standalone would be best on a street in a good location."

"Sounds great. I have all of your preferences."

"Thank you so much. Sorry to take you away from other projects."

Flora chuckled. "EJ is paying me well to ensure you get what you want."

"He shouldn't have. I could have found a place on my own."

"We both know EJ is stubborn," Flora replied.

"True, and speak of the devil, he's calling me."

"I'll call you in a few days."

"Thanks, Flora." I clicked the call to answer for EJ. "Hello?"

"When did you get home?"

"Are you looking at the cameras?"

"Have to keep up with you."

I laughed, chopping up the vegetables and placing them in the skillet. "How's work going?"

"Work is work. I wanted to hear your voice."

"I went to the store and came back to cook lunch."

"For who?"

"Mckayla's coming over with SJ."

"Do you need anything?"

"I scheduled a time with Flora to check out business locations for the clinic reopening."

"You don't have to rush back to work, Cora."

"I need to work. I need to take my mind off Julia."

EJ sighed. "I want you to give yourself a break."

I poured oil into the pan and stirred the vegetables. "You being here for me is enough."

"Tell Flora that the cost is irrelevant, and call me later if you need something on my way home."

"How late are you working?"

"Until I get confirmation of the retraction from the newspapers."

"And Enrique Vargas?"

"Our sources say he's flying back to Mexico."

"Make sure you come home to me."

I heard the front door open and close, and then SJ ran into the kitchen. "Let me call you back. They're here."

I ended the call and turned to pick up SJ. "Hi, little one."

"Hi, Cora." He laughed as I tickled his stomach.

Mckayla placed his toys on the island and grabbed the bottle of water from the fridge. I put SJ back on his feet and ruffled his hair.

"Do you need help with cooking?" Mckayla passed me the celery sticks, and I chopped them into a bowl.

"No. Tacos will be ready soon."

"Were you talking to Elio?"

"I was. He's at work."

"The girls wanted to come over, but he said to give you some time."

"I miss everybody, but he's right. I needed space for a little bit."

"Well, everyone except your nephew." Mckayla pointed at her nosy son, staring at us. We burst into laughter, and she nudged him to go play.

"My mom came by the other day, then EJ's parents."

"That's the nature of family. First the parents, then the in-laws," Mckayla joked.

I flipped the meat in the pan, lowered the heat, and turned to face her. "Sometimes I dream it was me who went back to the building instead of Julia," I confessed.

"We've all been there, Cora."

"She was a friend, not just a coworker."

Mckayla stood from the stool and embraced me. "You can't blame yourself. Have you talked with her family at all?"

"No. I tried calling them, but they blocked me once they found out who I was connected to."

"What happened to Colson and the other staff?"

"Some are too scared to return, but Colson is fine." I picked up a napkin to wipe my tears.

"Release your guilt and understand it won't hurt like this forever."

"Thanks, Mckayla."

"You're welcome. Now, let's eat and talk about how the trip."

"You still want to go?"

Mckayla laughed. "More than you know."

* * *

Mckayla told me to give Julia's family time to grieve, but I wanted to attend the funeral to pay my respects. I sat in the limousine wearing black shades and a large hat to hide as much of myself as possible. Anissa and Devi had come for moral support.

"You don't need to do this, you know," Devi said softly, holding my hand.

I sighed and stared out the tinted window at the crowd walking into the church. "If I don't, I'll regret it later."

"We can go inside whenever you're ready," Anissa said.

I wiped my tears away and closed my eyes to compose myself. Reaching the door, I stepped out, followed by Anissa and Devi. Both girls walked alongside me, holding my hands for support. I kept my head down to avoid any cameras or family recognizing me as we found seats near the door in the back of the church.

Anissa passed me an obituary, and I smiled at the images of Julia when she was younger. Anissa pointed out Julia's accomplishments as her family arrived and took their seats.

I felt a dark gaze on me and looked up to see Julia's mom.

"You have some nerve showing up here," she hissed.

"I'm sorry about what happened," I said quietly.

"You need to leave!" Julia's mother screamed.

"But I—"

She raised a hand to halt me. "My daughter is dead because of you."

"Honey, calm down." Julia's father tried to pull her away.

"Maybe we should go," Devi whispered.

I nodded and rose from my seat.

"Come near us again, and I'll call the police," Julia's mother warned.

I gasped in shock, suddenly realizing all eyes were on us.

"Come on, Cora. We need to leave," Anissa said.

"Anissa's right." Devi ran a hand across my shoulder.

Julia's mother reached out to grab me, but security moved between us.

"No! It's all right. She's upset," I barked at them.

"Trying to kill me like you did my daughter! Get out of here!" she yelled.

The incident caused a huge scene, and cameras flashed as I returned to the car.

"Drive!" I yelled as we all clambered inside and ducked down.

"That was crazy." Anissa tried to cover the windows with her arms as cameras flashed.

I could never have imagined someone close to me dying. I listened to Devi on the phone telling her husband what had happened as we pulled into the parking structure of my apartment.

My phone rang as soon as we stepped inside the apartment.

"Did she fucking touch you?" EJ barked.

"No. Calm down."

"I'm on my way to you now."

"No, everything is fine, EJ."

"Cora, you're not fine."

"She was upset. I shouldn't have gone in the first place."

He sighed, and the phone went silent. "Come home."

"Let me talk with the girls, and I'll be over to your place in a little bit."

"Don't be long."

"I promise."

"Cora?"

"Yeah?"

"It's not your fault."

"I know."

Anissa and Devi stayed with me. Anissa talked about her relationship issues with Mitchel, and I welcomed the subject change, enjoying the support from my friends. They left an hour later, and I went to EJ's house for the night.

Chapter 20

Elio Jr

I told Cora I'd give her space after the clean-up of her clinic and promised to help her get a new space, even though she refused my money. Today, I planned to surprise her with lunch and a trip to Paris, just the two of us.

Enrique hadn't returned to Mexico and was still in hiding, but Renato was running around the city to locate him and his crew. I'd instructed Cora's security detail to stay with her and the girls while they shopped today.

"Check this out," Vincenzo said.

"What?"

"I did some research and found out Enrique called a few of Cora's friends."

"Friends, like who?"

"Anissa. He must have tapped into her line and got her whereabouts during the past few weeks since the explosion."

I took the phone records and flipped through them, seeing he'd added software to trace calls and messages in their group chats. "He has Devi and Wale's information too."

Vincenzo picked up the phone, dialed a number, and put it on speaker. "Listen."

"*I want him dead. Her, too.*" Enrique's voice replayed.

"We discovered he's been stalking Julia's family and threatening to hurt them if they didn't give up information on Cora."

"He's not going to stop until we catch him."

"We need to make a move now. Anissa's boyfriend was seen talking to a nurse at the hospital, and she's connected to the Vargas Cartel." Vincenzo flipped through the photos.

"Motherfucker," I mumbled.

"Mitchel's an idiot. He gave up details about Anissa and Cora to a pretty face. Jessica Vargas. I'm surprised they haven't killed him yet," Vincenzo said.

My stomach dropped. I needed to get eyes on Cora. "Where is he now?"

"At the hospital."

"Let's go."

We passed Renato as we headed for the elevator. "What's the rush?"

"Mitchel is the connection."

The three of us stepped into the elevator and pulled out my phone to contact Cora as we reached the main lobby.

"She's not answering."

Freddie was waiting in the car, and we headed to the hospital to catch Jessica and Mitchel.

"Where's Cora right now?" Renato asked.

"She's supposed to be shopping." I dialed Cora's number and waited for her to answer. "She must be in place with no service. I told her to keep her phone on at all times."

It didn't take long to reach the memorial hospital. Renato directed Freddie to stay at the entrance, and we headed straight for the front desk in the emergency room.

"Where's Mitchel Blaine?"

"I'm sorry, sir, we can't give out that information."

I reached through the window and gripped the guy's collar, pulling his face close to mine. "Mitchel Blaine."

His eyes pleaded to be let go, and I squeezed harder.

He pointed toward the emergency exit. "Fourth floor."

We took the stairs to the fourth floor, and I saw Mitchel laughing with a girl.

"Mitchel!" I shouted, stalking toward him.

"EJ!"

I punched him in the face. "Where is she?"

Mitchel reeled back and clutched his jaw. "Who? I don't know anything."

"This girl." I held the picture up to his face.

His eyes ballooned wide. "I-I...don't know."

"How did you meet her?"

"She was here one night with a friend."

"What friend?" Vincenzo asked.

"Uh, I think one of her girlfriends was sick." He scratched his head and took a pained breath.

"Put your hands up!" Security barked, grabbing my shoulder to pull me off Mitchel.

I shoved them back. "Get the fuck off me!" I reached for my gun.

Vincenzo stalled me. "Not here. We need to go find Cora," he muttered.

I glared at Mitchel. "Call Anissa."

"She's out right now, and I have to get back to my patients."

I closed my eyes and counted to three. "Call... Anissa...now."

Vincenzo shoved Mitchel along with us as we left the hospital.

"I can't just leave," Mitchel pleaded.

I stopped, ready to put a bullet in his head for pissing me off, but settled for another punch to his jaw.

Vincenzo helped him to his feet. "You better pray Cora's fine."

I dialed Anissa's number, heading back to the car. Someone answered, and I could hear laughter in the background.

"Cora?" I called her name, and the line went dead.

"Take us to the mall," I instructed Freddie.

He started the car and headed into traffic.

My phone rang, and I looked down to see Constantine Hudson's name. "What does she

want?" I mumbled. I hit answer. "This isn't a good time, Constantine."

"Make the time. Come to the house. We need to get some things straightened out."

"Savio or Vincenzo can handle whatever you need."

"I don't doubt that, but we must get the papers signed today."

"I have a family emergency."

"The police came to see me," Constantine said.

"Why?"

"Wanting to know if I believed you hadn't killed Roy."

"Right now, I could care less what the police have to say about your asshole of a husband. Don't call me unless it's about paying off the rest of your husband's debt."

* * *

Vincenzo had his contacts working around the clock, and we'd pinpointed a hotel where Enrique might be staying.

I checked my gun's chamber before jumping out of the car and heading into the hotel. Vincenzo jogged beside me, and we left Mitchel with Freddie. We rushed inside, ignoring the calls of hotel security, and pushed in front of other guests to get on the elevator. I flashed my gun and pushed the button for floor nineteen. I tapped my gun against my thigh, itching to slice the Vargas family into little pieces and throw Mitchel in the same pile. The elevator dinged softly, and we moved down the hallway until we located room 221.

I pressed my ear against the door. "Stand back."

Vincenzo grasped me by the shoulder as I raised my gun. "We can't shoot into a hotel room."

"Fuck this hotel." I barked.

He moved me out of the way and attached his silencer. Aiming, he fired at the door handle, and it popped open. I kicked it open, my gun at the ready, only to be greeted by silence.

"He's running," Vincenzo said, moving into the room.

A foul smell wafted around the room from the trash, and day-old food was lying on the table. Using the gun's tip to move around the clothes, my eyes narrowed on the empty ashtray with ashes scattered around it. Red lipstick coated the end of a half-smoked cigarette.

"They must have just left." I whirled and went to the bathroom. Steam from the shower still coated the walls, and towels were strewn on the floor. A message was written in the condensation on the mirror.

"*She's next,*" I murmured out loud.

"Anything in here?" Vincenzo rounded the corner.

"They're going after Cora." Fire coursed through my bloodstream.

"Time we called for help."

My phone vibrated with a message from Renato.

Renato: *Bring Mitchel to the warehouse.*

Me: *Cora's not answering her phone.*

Renato: *What was her last location?*

Me: *She said she was going to the mall.*

Renato: *We can ping her phone.*

Me: *Send it to me soon as you get a hit.*

I looked at Freddie. "Take us to the warehouse."

"Is that a good idea?" Freddie asked. "Mitchel is Anissa's boyfriend, and Anissa is Cora's best friend."

"Anissa will find someone else. I'm doing her a favor by taking out the trash."

I looked at Mitchel, unconscious in the backseat. From what Cora had told me, he was always flirting and had hooked up with other girls behind Anissa's back.

I dialed Marilyn's number.

"Hi, EJ." She answered on the first ring.

"Hey, Marilyn. I'm calling to see if Cora's with you."

"No. I haven't heard from her all day," Marilyn replied.

"If you do, tell her to go straight home and wait for me."

Marilyn's voice hiked in nervousness. "Anything I should be worried about? You sound like something's wrong."

The minute I spilled about Cora being missing, Marilyn would tell my parents, and they would get involved. The fewer people who knew, the safer Cora would be. "No problem. Just have her call me as soon as possible."

"I will, EJ. Call me if you hear from her."

I assured her I would and ended the call.

On the way to the mall, Freddie made a detour, stopping at our warehouse. Renato motioned for his team to move Mitchel into the warehouse, and we switched cars.

"Savio's going to meet us if he can," I said as we climbed into the black escalade with Renato and Vincenzo.

The knot in my chest continued to grow the longer I didn't know Cora's whereabouts.

Renato grinned. "Let's ride."

Chapter 21

Cora

"I think we need to figure out a new location," I told Anissa on the phone as I left the meeting with the real estate agent.

Elio had fought me on using someone outside of his family's firm, but I had the independence to choose myself. I'd planned to go shopping with the girls, but Flora could only get me in to see the place today because she had another viewing and a potential buyer.

"Each location will have unique selling points, so take your time, Cora," Flora said with a smile as she locked up the building.

I froze as something cold and hard pressed against my back.

"Don't move," a familiar voice instructed.

Everything happened in slow motion as Enrique raised his gun and shot Flora in the head.

"Flora!" I screamed, fighting frantically against his hold. "Why are you doing this?" I sobbed.

Enrique grabbed my hair and pushed me toward the door. "Don't question me."

He dragged me out of the building and down the stairs. My two guards were dead in the car.

"No! Let me go!"

Enrique ignored my cries and pushed me toward the Mercedes. I stumbled and fell, and he lifted me by the back of my neck, tossing me onto the backseat. "Put on your seatbelt," he hissed.

I reached for the door immediately, but he yanked me back and pushed the gun under my chin.

"You want to die today, Cora? Keep fighting me." He ran the gun down my throat and across my chest.

I smacked his hand away, and he retaliated by hitting me across the face. I cried out and fell back.

His henchman spoke. "The plane is ready, Mr. Vargas."

"Hurry before he finds out she's gone," Enrique answered.

I whimpered, hunched in the backseat as the landscape sped past, praying Elio found me soon.

Enrique answered his ringing phone, talking so fast I struggled to make sense of what he was saying.

"My brother is dead, and you want me to let it go?"

Enrique glared at me. My end was near, and I wished EJ knew how much I loved him. I should have agreed to move in together. We'd lost so much time since we broke up, and all the fighting seemed pointless now.

The driver headed into the Chicago tunnel, and I briefly considered jumping out. I'd rather die at my own hands than get on a flight to Mexico with Enrique.

"Enrique, please let me go," I pleaded.

"Why would I let such a prize leave?" Enrique shoved the gun under my chin again.

"Elio and I aren't together anymore. I'm of no value to you," I reasoned.

He chuckled as he caressed my cheek, and I flinched away.

"Oh shit!" the driver said suddenly, swerving around an oncoming car.

"Let me out of here!" I screamed, trying to open the door again.

The other car turned with a squeal of tires. It sped up, and the occupants started shooting at us.

"Get us out of here now!" Enrique yelled.

I ducked down and covered my head as bullets flew around us. My heart was beating out of my chest.

One of the guards passed Enrique an automatic weapon. Glass shattered around us as we were hit from behind.

"Fuck! Boss, we're trapped," Enrique's guard informed him.

I peered out to see cars on either side of us and one behind. We were boxed in. What if someone was after Enrique and I was killed simply for being in his car? So many mob wars started over the littlest thing.

Enrique snatched me by the arm and shoved the door open. He dragged me out and planted his gun against my temple. "You think I'm afraid to kill her?"

I gasped when I saw EJ staring back at us, his gun in his hand. "EJ!" I yelled, struggling against Enrique's hold.

He pressed forcefully against my cheek.

"Cora, remember what I said?" EJ called.

"No talking! You killed my brother, so it's only fair I kill your bitch!"

"Don't be stupid, Enrique," Sante yelled.

EJ moved a little closer.

"Stay back!" Enrique removed the gun from my cheek and aimed at EJ.

"No!" I yelled, throwing myself at him.

Enrique pulled the trigger. I dropped to the ground, and his body jerked as bullets flew.

"Cora!" EJ shouted.

I looked up hesitantly to see him running toward me. Dropping beside me, he searched me frantically for any wounds.

"I've got you, baby," he said, lifting me bridal-style.

I wrapped my arms around his neck, buried my face in his chest, and sobbed.

"Vincenzo? Shit, Vincenzo's hit!" Sante yelled.

Sirens blared in the distance as EJ placed me in the backseat of his car and rushed to check on his brother.

My eyes widened with horror as I saw Enrique staggering toward EJ. He was holding his stomach, and his gun was clutched in his hand.

"EJ! Look out!" I screamed, pointing behind him.

Enrique's face was twisted with an evil smirk. Blood seeped from his stomach wound and trickled from his mouth. "All this blood is on your hands," he spat, lifting his gun toward EJ and pulling the trigger.

It jammed.

EJ charged toward him with a roar, knocking him to the ground. Sante raced over and pulled EJ off Enrique before he put another bullet in him. Enrique was dead, and no part of me regretted it.

"Let's go. Too many eyes out here," Sante urged, pushing EJ into the car with me.

I threw myself at him, cupping his face in my hands. "I don't know what I would have done if you'd left me."

EJ pulled me onto his lap and wrapped his arms

around me. "I'll never leave you, Cora. Not so long as I'm drawing breath."

The police and paramedics arrived, and we watched as they loaded an injured Vincenzo onto a stretcher and into the back of the ambulance. A few of the Calabresi Cartel shook hands with the police officers, and I knew that meant they were on the payroll.

As Freddie started the car and we followed behind the ambulance, I knew Enrique could no longer hurt anyone I loved.

* * *

"Cora! Are you okay?" My mom rushed into the bedroom at EJ's house and hugged me.

I grabbed my mother's hand, planted it on my cheek, and smiled. "I'm fine, promise."

EJ had insisted I be checked out at the hospital, but I was fine compared to Vincenzo. It was more important that EJ cared for his family and was there for them instead of stuck with me. She smothered me in her arms.

"What happened? EJ didn't tell me anything other than to get here quickly," Mom said, her expression concerned.

"Enrique Vargas kidnapped me when I was looking at another location for my clinic."

"Oh, my God. Did he hurt you?"

The idea of what he could have done if given a chance made me nauseous. "No. EJ got there in time. I'm more worried about Vincenzo."

The door opened, and Mckayla, Rena, and Anissa entered with the kids.

"We came to cheer you up," Mckayla said, helping SJ onto the bed.

I smiled and rubbed SJ's head. "Thanks, Mckayla. I won't be good until I hear how Vincenzo's doing."

"Adelina's at the hospital. I'll call her and get an update," Mom said. She kissed my cheek and left the room.

I rested my head against the pillow with a weary sigh.

Rena sat on the end of the bed with her phone in her hand. "I'm checking with Sante now."

"I hate to say it, but welcome to the club." Mckayla took a seat on the chaise lounge.

"What club?" I yawned.

"Being the woman of a Calabresi man is dangerous. No matter how hard we try to stay out of their business, it finds us."

I listened as Mckayla and Rena shared stories of how they'd had to deal with life-and-death situations. It was why I'd tried not to fall in love with EJ.

"No word yet. Sante said they're still working on Vincenzo," Rena announced, still texting on her phone. "Enrique thought he could kill a Calabresi boss, but that will never happen." Rena winked at me.

I grinned. "Too late to regret falling in love now. Seeing them in action, protecting their loved ones is humbling."

Mckayla sighed. "We need a vacation as soon as Vincenzo is on the mend."

"A vacation sounds great, but I want to get my business back up and running, and ...Oh, my God! Flora!" I clapped a hand over my mouth as I suddenly remembered Enrique shooting her.

"Who?" Rena asked.

"Flora, the real estate agent. I need to call EJ." I tried to climb out of bed, but Mckayla held me back.

"Calm down. You're recovering from a shootout."

"Flora was showing me a new building when Enrique kidnapped me." I rubbed my forehead.

"Do you remember the location?" Mckayla removed her phone from her pocket.

I closed my eyes to recall the address. "Um, it was about twenty minutes from the Holland Tunnel." I climbed out of bed and started to dress.

"Cora, you can't go off by yourself. EJ will kill us," Mckayla reasoned.

"Then drive me to the area. I feel so bad. Flora was a sweet woman and didn't deserve what happened."

"EJ will send Freddie," Rena said.

I snapped my fingers as I remembered I'd written down the address. I grabbed my purse off the dresser, pulled out the balled-up paper, and handed it to Mckayla.

"You need to eat and shower," she said.

"Food can wait." My stomach grumbled as I pulled out a clean pair of shorts and a T-shirt.

"Your stomach says differently. Go shower and get some rest. We'll order you some food, and Freddie will check on the address."

"Thanks, Mckayla." I hugged her close.

"We're sisters. Light some candles and take a long bath. Food will be here soon," Rena said.

Mckayla gathered the kids up to leave, and I waved goodbye. I went to the bathroom and shut the door behind me, leaning against the door.

"Welcome to the club," I mumbled.

* * *

Light snores and a strong arm draped over my waist woke me. I turned on the lamp. "EJ?"

He kissed the back of my head. "Go back to sleep."

"How is Vincenzo?"

EJ opened one eye. "He's fine. My father moved him to a private facility to keep it under wraps."

"What happens now?"

"We're going to move in together and get married."

"I mean, about your business and the cartel?"

"I never talk business, Cora."

"EJ, don't treat me like an outsider."

A fire sparked in his eyes. "Business will run as usual."

"But I saw the police surrounding the area, and I doubt all of them are on the payroll."

"Stop worrying."

I checked the time. It was almost two am. "When did you get here?"

He released a tight breath. "An hour ago."

"Are you hungry?"

"Not for food." He drew me closer.

"Do you want to talk about what happened today?" My hand slipped to the back of his neck.

He nuzzled his nose against my neck. "Do you feel safe with me?"

"Of course I do. We could have avoided this mess if I hadn't kept you at a distance."

"It would've happened at some point." He pressed his lips to mine.

I moaned into his mouth. "You're everything, EJ."

He slipped my shirt over my head and stared at my naked body. I stretched my legs wide for him, and he bit his bottom lip.

"No more distance. We discuss any problems and listen to each other," he said huskily.

"I agree. I'm sorry for listening to Enrique."

"Enrique used you to get to me. He won't be bothering us anymore."

Elio slipped a hand between my thighs, pushed a finger into my center, and I crumbled underneath him. His lips crashed into mine, and his tongue licked the seam of my mouth.

I grasped his thick length and rubbed my thumb over his tip. "Make love to me."

"That's all I've ever wanted to do."

His words branded my heart. I would always belong to him.

EJ trailed kisses down my body until he was positioned between my thighs. He gripped my hips, and I cried out his name as his tongue darted across my clit. Another swipe sent me hurtling over the edge. Wanting more, he lifted my leg over his shoulder and dove deeper.

"Show me what belongs to you," I panted.

He crawled up my body, his eyes burning with intent. My back arched as he slid inside me, stretching me and hitting my G-spot. I moaned as he bent to suckle my nipples. Our sweet connection overwhelmed me, and tears trembled on my lashes.

"EJ," I whispered, my voice trembling.

"God, you feel so good. Wanna come in your pussy, baby."

"Yes! I'm coming," I gasped, arching my back as my orgasm crept up my spine and exploded in my core.

We made love for hours. His arms were my home, and I never wanted to leave.

Chapter 22

Elio Jr

Memories of the EMTs placing my brother into the ambulance haunted me. I felt guilty for dragging him into my mess with Enrique. My family was used to Renato and Savio having problems with enemies since one was the enforcer and the other was the Don of the family. Being the lawyer, I usually stayed under the radar.

The fear in Cora's eyes as Enrique held the gun to her head had almost destroyed me. If I'd died protecting her, it would have been worth it. Enrique thought kidnapping Cora would bring me to my knees, but it only stoked the fire in my belly that demanded I kill him.

The water from the shower cascaded down my back, washing away the aches from all the running and fighting. Cora got up an hour ago despite me trying to keep her in bed. She wanted to cook breakfast for the family.

There would be no more secrets between Cora and me. Learning about the miscarriage had almost broken me. I wanted Cora to know she could share everything with me, good and bad.

I told her I was heading to check on Vincenzo and talk to my father about what the Vargas Cartel was going to do.

I dried off after my shower and brushed my teeth. Dressing casually in slacks and a T-shirt. I heard laughing from the kitchen and entered to see Cora and SJ at the island placing pancakes on plates.

I ruffled SJ's hair and kissed the back of Cora's neck. Picking up a piece of bacon, I tossed it into my mouth.

"Are you heading to check on Vincenzo?" Rena took the glass of orange juice from Marilyn.

I picked up a coffee cup and waited for her to pour some for Mckayla. "Yes. Mom and Dad are waiting for me to get there before they leave."

"How is he doing?" Rena pinned her gaze on me.

"He's going to be fine."

Cora looked up at me and back to her plate.

"I promise, he's fine. A bullet to his leg and shoulder."

"What are you girls up to today?" Rena asked Cora, helping SJ to cut up his pancakes.

"I wanted to see Flora's family and give my condolences."

We'd already set aside enough money to cover the burial costs and secure her kids' future.

"I'm sure her family will appreciate your condolences," I said. "I want you to think about moving in here."

"Already decided." Cora's eyes rested on me.

"Really? No pushback?"

Cora stood from her seat and wrapped her arms around my waist. "No. You almost got shot, plus the situation with Vincenzo made me realize I don't want to waste another second of my time with you."

"I agree with your answers, Mrs. Calabresi."

She chuckled at me calling her my wife. "No ring yet. We still have time before we start talking weddings."

"Once you live with him for six months, you'll be ready to get married." Rena laughed, and I threw a grape at her head.

Cora giggled, and I kissed her again before leaving the house.

* * *

Freddie drove to the private medical facility close to my parent's estate. I listened to Cora discuss her plans to re-open her business once she found another building.

"Babe, let me call you back."

"Tell your parents hello, and that I'll visit soon."

"I will." I ended the call.

It was good to know that Cora finally had no doubts about us. She had accepted my love and realized that my protectiveness wasn't to keep her under my thumb but to show how far I would go to keep her safe and loved.

Once at the facility, I went straight to Vincenzo's room. Renato was sitting in the chair with his feet up on Vincenzo's bed like he lived there. I slapped his feet down, and Vincenzo chuckled. It was good to see him laughing and relaxed.

"How are you feeling?"

Vincenzo rested his hand on his stomach. "Better,"

"He looks like a man who got shot." Renato smirked.

"Is everything with the Vargas Cartel complet-ed?" Vincenzo asked, ignoring Renato.

"He's been put to rest. No more brothers knocking on my door."

Renato cracked his knuckles. "Maybe I should go find the mother and take out the cause of her bastard kids."

"For now, we leave it alone. Cacho wants a truce, so we're meeting with him today."

"I want to be there," Vincenzo announced.

"You need to worry about getting better," I said.

His face scrunched up. "It's a flesh wound."

"Doesn't matter. You know Ma insists you stay out of the business."

Vincenzo grumbled, "She has to learn I'm not a baby anymore."

"What time is the meeting with Cacho?" Renato asked.

I looked at my watch. "In an hour."

Renato pushed Vincenzo back down as he tried to sit up. "I will kill you myself before I let Adelina come at me about her precious baby boy getting hurt again."

I knew Vincenzo hated being treated like a baby, but our parents expected us to look out for him.

"Yeah, right," Vincenzo scoffed.

As I talked with him about what the doctors expected for his recovery, the nurse checked his vitals.

"Mr. Calabresi, are you hungry?" she asked.

She was short with blonde hair, red pouty lips, and a full figure. She was just the kind of woman Vincenzo would take home for the night under normal circumstances.

"I'd love something hot and spicy, Natalia." Vincenzo grinned at her.

"Be good, Mr. Calabresi, and I might bring you steak and pasta." She checked his blood pressure and fixed his pillow.

"When can he be released?" I asked Natalia.

"The doctor recommended another few days as a precaution," Natalia answered.

"Make sure we have a guard up here with him," I told Renato.

"Already done," Renato replied.

We sat with Vincenzo for another twenty minutes before leaving to finish our business with the Vargas underboss.

* * *

Cacho sat with his legs crossed and a bottle of nineteen forty-two as a gift to show he came in peace. To my mind, peace meant having his entire family wiped out, but business didn't work out the way I wanted.

"Tell us why we should continue to agree to a truce." I led the conversation with Cacho while his guards stood behind him.

Izan and Enrique would have been with him if they'd understood how things worked.

"I want to apologize for what happened to your brother and woman. I'd like to offer ten percent of sales, plus the route will be undetected by any *policia* or agents."

"Ten percent won't compensate for how your brothers hurt my family."

Cacho's mouth twisted. "Fifteen."

"Fifty percent, plus we put our people in Mexico."

"That's bullshit." Cacho jabbed his finger on the table.

"Enrique started the war. We just finished it. Take the offer or go back to Mexico with nothing."

Cacho scanned Renato, Savio, and me. "Does he

speak for the entire cartel and you as the Boss?" He waved at Savio.

"Testing me as the Don will only put you in a body bag. Elio gave you the terms." Savio backed me up, showing our loyalty to each other.

"I need to speak with my family," Cacho finally said.

I opened my briefcase and removed a document, placing it on the table along with a gun.

"You have two choices. Fifty percent, or you leave in a body bag like your brothers."

Cacho bowed his head. I pushed the legal document in front of him with a pen. He signed his name, giving us fifty percent of their sales under our corporation's name so it couldn't be traced back. The legit real estate and construction business came in handy as we built new properties in Mexico.

"Glad you made the right decision."

Cacho rose and leaned over the table with a menacing glare. "None of my investors will like this outcome."

Making a deal he hadn't consulted on with his people would get him killed before he stepped foot back in Mexico.

"Then I suggest you find a new home, but Chicago is not it, Mr. Vargas."

Cacho straightened his jacket and turned, and left the office.

"Nice way to do business, brother." Renato proudly shook my hand.

"File those papers and put a percent under charity," Savio said.

"How is Cora feeling?" Sante inquired.

"I left her with the girls. She seems good now."

"The more you keep her apprised of what's happening, the better. After what Rena went through, I kept in touch every day, so she wasn't afraid something would happen again."

"Same with Mckayla," Savio replied.

"Sonya and my son stayed at my hip," Renato responded and lit a cigar.

"I asked her to move in with me."

Renato grinned. "Should have done that years ago."

"Are you prepared for a real relationship and the responsibilities?" Savio tried to be the father and big brother when it came to women. Ironically, he'd been the biggest whore before he got with Mckayla.

"Remember, I had a girlfriend before any of you." I tilted my chin at each brother.

"Then you broke up with her and made her watch you move on with other women," Savio jested.

I glared at him. "That's in the past. We've talked about everything."

Renato slapped the back of my head and headed for the door with Sante. "Don't hurt her again, or you will answer to me, lover boy."

I didn't have a comeback before the door closed behind them.

Savio winked at me. "She's special."

"I know."

"Mom wants you to marry her."

My cheeks heated. "We haven't gotten there yet, but she's my future."

He pursed his lips. "That's what I like to hear, little brother."

"Thanks. We need to hurry for family dinner."

"Vincenzo comes home soon, and we'll have a big party."

"He's getting more anxious to be on the cartel side."

Savio chuckled. "Mother will kill me."

"I told him already, but he wants to be more active."

Savio shook his head. "I can talk to him again."

"He's doing better. I felt guilty about Enrique shooting him."

"Vincenzo's no dummy, but we need to prepare if that moment comes."

"I'll catch up with you at the family dinner. I need to head over to the office and get these papers filed."

Savio clapped me on the back. "Call me if you need me."

* * *

"I saw on the news that your girlfriend is safe." Constantine sat in the chair opposite my desk.

"That's not why you're here, so leave the pleasantries to someone who cares."

"Business all the time, Mr. Calabresi."

"Not when it becomes personal."

Constantine's nostrils flared. "Here's the final payment of my husband's debt." She placed a check on my desk next to papers of hotel construction groundbreaking clearance from the county.

"Will that check bounce?"

"Unlike my husband, I back up what I say."

"That's going to take time."

"Percentage is still fifteen from the casino and five from the hotel?"

"That was never the deal. Casino ten percent, and we provide you with funding for reelection support."

Constantine's eyes locked on mine. "I have to provide

for my family, and a casino is a fickle business. I should be provided with more, considering the number of licenses I'm overlooking."

"I have no clue what you're talking about, Acting Governor Hudson."

Constantine huffed and leaned forward in her chair. She picked up the pen on my desk and signed her name on the dotted line. "I'll be sure to be the first at the front door when you open." Constantine turned and left my office.

"Bitch." I asked my assistant to come and dictate notes on my upcoming schedule and get the check sent over to Renato for clearance.

Chapter 23

Cora

Weeks had passed since Enrique had kidnapped me. I'd spoken with Flora's family, who were grateful for the flowers and money the Calabresi family had sent to her kids.

I finally felt like my old self again and put my energy into getting my business up and running again. EJ supported my decision and told me that whatever I needed would be provided. He'd had his team find me a new location, so I went with Anissa to check it out. It was still under construction and needed a lot of work. I'd planned on being here morning and night to get it exactly how I wanted it.

Freddie parked the car, and when I glanced out the window, my mouth gaped in surprise.

"What has he done?" A tingle pricked my arms.

Anissa cracked up beside me.

"Did you know about him doing this?" I wagged my finger at the surprise sign on the building with balloons.

"Yes. He wanted to keep it under wraps." Anissa unlocked the car door and stepped out.

EJ had gone above and beyond this time, creating exactly what I'd envisioned for my clinic. "When did he have time?"

Anissa gripped my hand and pulled me toward the door. A large sign with my name hung above the door with the opening hours, and pictures of kids with their animals hung on the walls just inside the entrance.

EJ was waiting inside, along with family and friends.

I ran to him as he opened his arms. "You did this for me?"

He kissed me. "Of course. Don't cry."

"Happy tears. And I'm paying you back."

He shook his head. I was stubborn, and it drove him crazy that I would never let him pay for anything. Being independent meant a lot to me, but there were some things I didn't fight him on.

Our parents talked in the corner, and his brothers crowded around their wives. This place was beautiful, with the decorations on the walls, and the entrance was much larger than my previous location. There was a refreshment counter and a section where the animals could gather and play. In the future, I dreamed about having multiple locations and creating somewhere that wasn't just a healing place for animals but a spa where the owners could send their pets to stay while on vacation.

"Do you like the place?" EJ pulled me in front of him, and I looped my arms around his neck.

"Are you kidding me? I love everything."

"Good, because I'm taking you on vacation before you return to work."

My brain ran off a list of things to prepare for opening a new business. "I can't. I need to hire staff, start training, and figure out a schedule."

"All of that can wait. You and I need some time alone." EJ wrapped his arms around my waist.

"But—"

"Shush. You worry too much. Besides, we still need to figure out your living arrangements."

I didn't argue with him. Staying at his place felt like home, and waking up in his arms gave me stability.

I tipped my head to the side. "Where were you thinking we could go?"

EJ grinned. "Bora Bora."

"Sounds exciting." My heart did cartwheels at the idea.

He tapped me on the nose. "Anything to get you alone and naked."

"Is that all you want me for?" I joked.

"That, and for you to carry my child one day."

"I should've told you about the baby. I'm so sorry I kept it from you."

"Never apologize. We were so young. I know you were hurt and confused. My mother and father made me see my faults."

"I'm thinking of seeing a therapist," I blurted out.

"If you think it will help, I support you."

"Maybe you can come with me sometimes." I didn't know if this concession would make or break our relationship.

"Baby steps, Cora." He chuckled, and my head fell back in laughter.

"Cora, thank God you came back because EJ was driving us insane," Renato joked, joining us with Rena.

Rena elbowed him in the stomach. "Like you weren't groveling with Sonya."

"Where is your husband again?" Renato growled.

Rena and I giggled as he marched back to Sonya in a huff.

I shook my head in disbelief. "He's the last person to talk about being insane."

EJ reached for my hand and squeezed. "I need to check in with my brothers. You good?"

"Great. Go take care of business."

Anissa and Rena stood with me as I watched EJ head off to talk with Savio and Sante.

"Did EJ tell you about Cacho and the Mexico deal?" Rena asked.

"No, what happened?"

"He forced them to sign over fifty percent to the Calabresi Cartel, or they would have killed him."

I knew there was something more to the news reports that Underboss Cacho Vargas had been found dead in his car from smoke inhalation.

"EJ never told me about what happened with them to end the war."

"I overheard Sante talking with his brothers," Rena said.

I knew she would hear about any business details because she sneaked around Sante's conversations.

"Whatever they did means you're safe for good. No more crazy killers after you and the family," Anissa said.

I grimaced. "I still can't believe Mitchel."

"Me neither. I was ready to marry him and discover all these secret dealings and mafia life." Anissa rolled her eyes.

"I'm glad you got out sooner than later," I said, hugging her.

Rena snapped her fingers. "I want to go out tonight."

Anissa grinned. "That would be fun. I need a night out with the girls."

I groaned. "I want to get started on work."

Rena waved her hand in my face. "Work can wait. You have plenty of time to get organized. We need to celebrate you and EJ back together."

"I agree." Anissa chimed in.

"Fine, but no strippers."

Rena winked at me. "Strippers can wait for the wedding."

* * *

"Mckayla couldn't come. The kids are sick," Rena yelled over the music from the DJ.

I listened to Beyonce's Cuff It play through the club. It gave me an idea to wake EJ up and give him the best night of his life when I got home later.

As usual, Freddie and Jason tagged along with us. They were probably annoyed at how often we'd dragged them out with us. EJ had a case to work on tonight, so he'd stayed home and told me to have fun. I never thought I'd see the day he wasn't all over me about what I was wearing or trying to peel it off my body. Rena thought it would be cute to wear leather, so I slipped on a leather and gold beaded dress that hiked my breasts up and gave my ass a little more cushion.

"Here, your hand should not be empty tonight." Rena poured me a glass of champagne.

I took the glass from her, and she raised hers for a toast.

"To Cora, for being a boss bitch who doesn't take crap

from anyone but keeps it classy with a sweet and kind heart."

I chuckled at her over-the-top descriptions. "You have to be with a Calabresi man."

"Here! Here! To Cora." Anissa gulped her drink down.

"I want to toast you, ladies, for supporting and being there for me."

"To me!" Rena clinked glasses with me, and I burst into laughter.

"All right, time to dance." Anissa rose and grabbed my hand. We danced in the VIP section while the DJ changed the beat to a throwback Christina Aguilera.

I cheered on Anissa and Rena, waved my hands, and moved my hips from side to side. I felt like I was in another dimension, free to let my hair down. All was right in the world.

I tensed as strong hands wrapped around my waist.

"Keep dancing like that, and you'll end up in the back of my car with your legs in the air."

I grinned at the deep familiar voice and turned my head to see a smirk on EJ's face. "What happened to working late?"

"I finished and wanted to come to celebrate with my baby."

"Or trying to keep tabs?"

"Both."

I laughed and danced in front of him as he watched. I planned to give him a show in the bedroom tonight that he'd never had before.

"You keep pushing your ass against me, see what happens." He grasped the back of my neck, and I purposely rolled my ass against his dick one more time.

"Get a room for you two!" Anissa shouted.

I laughed and took EJ by the hand, tugging him from the VIP section and down the hall to the exit.

"Are you leaving with me?"

I turned to face him before we got to the car. "What do you think?" I stood on my tiptoes and slipped my tongue into his mouth, dropping my hand and squeezing his dick. He instantly hardened at my touch.

"Is that a yes to moving with me?" he asked raggedly.

"Yes," I purred as his tongue trailed down my throat.

He yanked the door open, and I climbed in with him right behind me. He pushed my dress up around my hips.

"EJ!" I cooed as his cool breath fanned across my lower lips through my panties.

"Pure, sweet, sexy baby."

"We should wait until we get home."

"Say it again." He sucked in on my inner thigh.

"Wait...until...w-we get h-home," I stuttered.

"You sure?"

"Oh, God, EJ!"

He ripped off my panties and slid a finger inside me. I crumbled at his touch as he moved his finger in and out.

"Come here." He hovered over me and planted a kiss on my lips that took my breath away. He'd teased, courted, and ignited me over the years. I'd always be grateful for the way our love had grown. I was excited about the future we would create together.

EJ lifted me to straddle his lap, and we gazed into each other's eyes. I didn't care if anyone saw us making love in the back of a car. It spiced things up even more.

"You remember the park we used to go to when we were younger and carved our names in the tree?"

He smiled and pushed me down onto his rod. "Fuck, Cora. I remember."

"We made a promise to be together forever."

He bit my neck lightly. "Mmhmm..."

I rolled my hips. "Let's go to that park tonight."

His eyes popped open at my request. "The park where you stormed out on me when I tried to ask you on our first date?"

I pouted. "I won't storm out this time. I want to reminisce."

"Anything for you." He moved me to the side of him and fixed himself up before knocking on the window to get Freddie's attention. "Let's go."

Freddie climbed behind the wheel and started the car, and EJ gave him directions to Grant Park. I rested my head on his shoulder as we headed for one of my favorite places. Minutes later, we stopped, and I looked out the window and smiled. It was around eleven at night, so people being out wasn't an issue.

I waited as EJ opened my door and walked me along the trail to our spot. He pushed me against the tree, and I wrapped my legs around his waist as he slipped inside my pussy.

"EJ!" I moaned as our bodies moved together. There was nothing like a spontaneous sex session at the place you'd agreed to be someone's girlfriend at fifteen.

"Cora, you've been mine forever."

"Baby, right there."

He tugged my dress down to expose my breasts and flicked his tongue over my nipples, sucking on my exposed skin.

My back arched off the tree, and I held him tighter. "I promise to love you for the rest of our lives."

"Hey!"

My head whipped around at the voice. I giggled as I saw the policeman holding a flashlight, trying to determine where the noises were coming from.

"Baby, there's a cop."

"Fuck that. Give him a show."

"EJ!" I screamed when he spread my ass and pumped faster and faster.

"What are you doing?" the officer demanded.

EJ ignored him, continuing to fuck me until we released together. The officer finally reached us as EJ helped me to stand, nudging me behind him protectively.

"Mr. Calabresi! I didn't know that was you." The officer fumbled over his words.

"Is there a problem, officer?" EJ asked.

"No problem at all, Mr. Calabresi. I just thought I heard a disturbance."

"Just me and my girl. You mind putting the flashlight away?"

"Routine, sir. You be safe out here," the officer said before walking away.

I slapped EJ on the back. "We almost got caught."

"He's not stupid. Let's go home and get you to bed." EJ curled his hand around mine.

"Tonight was great." I peered up at him.

He grinned. "Plenty more to come."

Chapter 24

Elio Jr

The welcome home party for my brother became more of a family reunion, with cousins from New York popping in and my mom inviting some of her relatives from Italy. My father didn't like a lot of people at our estate, but he couldn't argue with my mom when she wanted something.

Cora stood off with a few of her coworkers and Anissa, laughing with the kids near the pool. Vincenzo stood with some chick he'd invited who wasn't his girlfriend but friends with one of our mom's close friends.

My mom came up to me. "How long are you going to stand in the same place?"

"Just scoping out the scene."

"Why don't I believe you? You look like someone who doesn't trust large groups and wants to protect his family."

"How do you know that?"

"Because your father is the same way," she said, pointing to my father, glaring at everyone. The old man was still vibrant. The cartel life would always be in his blood.

"Can't fault us for wanting to keep you safe."

"Oh, no, it's not me you're keeping safe. I saw that look on your face when Cora was talking to your cousin, Bosco.

My mouth twitched. "It was a look of contentment at having the most beautiful woman in the world."

My mother's eyes gleamed as she laughed. "No, it was the "I will murder you if you touch my woman" look. Bosco knows Cora belongs to you."

"Good, but I'm never worried."

"Nice to know you've evolved and will hopefully give me some grandbabies."

I waved a hand at the crowd of kids near the pool. "You already have grandbabies."

"I want enough to fill each room in the house."

I smirked. "That's my plan."

"Cora loves you, and I'm happy you two have reconnected."

"It wasn't about reconnecting. It was about letting her have fun before I locked it down."

"There's that macho Calabresi blood."

I shrugged. "Dad did the same with you."

"He did, and at first, I wanted to piss him off by dating other people, but our relationship dynamic is different from you and Cora."

"Cora's always been the one."

"I can see it in your eyes."

The fire in my belly could only be drowned with Cora's love. "Thank you for helping get her business up and running again."

"All I did was make some phone calls for my daughter-in-law."

"She agreed to move in with me." The thrill of us together at my place warmed my heart.

Mom sighed. "From the moment she walked into our house all those years ago, I could see you two had something."

"See? Bosco seems to think I'm the nice cousin," I murmured when I saw him hugging Cora. He turned to wink at me.

Mom laughed, and I stomped off to go fuck him up for trying me.

"My cousin has a jealous streak, Cora," Bosco murmured, and the other girls laughed at him.

Cora came to stand between us. "Stop being grouchy and kiss me."

Bosco raised his hands in the air. "Cousin, you worry too much."

"Fuck you, Bosco." I glowered at him.

A chuckle escaped his lips, and I flipped him off.

"Are you having a good time?" Cora asked.

I grabbed the cup from her hand and took a gulp. "Yeah. You all right?"

"Great. Having fun with your family."

"Bro, you need to talk to Mom. She's trying to hook me up with Glenda's daughter," Vincenzo grumbled, hiding behind Cora and me.

"Who?"

Vincenzo pointed at our mother and Glenda near the food table, whispering to each other.

"What happened to the girl you came to the party with?"

"She tried to slip past Mom to the bathroom, and Mom accused her of being a prostitute."

"Is she?"

Cora slapped me on the chest. "Don't call her that."

I slumped my shoulders. "You're right."

Vincenzo smirked because we both knew he had an appetite for hiring escorts and one-night stands.

"What the hell was Bosco talking to you about?"

Cora shook her head. "Nothing."

"Cora—"

"Seriously, he was pretending to talk to me to make you jealous."

I smacked her on the ass and huffed, "Family."

"Come and get some food with me." Cora took my hand and guided me away from the girls and my brother.

Cora lifted a plate and started to add everything from fruit and salad to burgers and hot dogs. I picked up another beer and whispered I'd be right back before heading inside to see what my father was doing.

I knocked on his office door but didn't wait for him to call me inside. "You're not coming outside?"

He removed his glasses and sat back in his chair. "Long as your mother is happy with her party."

"What's the problem, old man?" I shut the door and took a seat in front of his desk.

"The Mexican government is interested in Cacho's death."

I shrugged. "We had nothing to do with his death."

Father glared. "As a lawyer, you know better."

"It was on American soil. Let the authorities deal with the cleanup."

My father paused, staring out of the window. "Cora has come out of her shell." His eyes crinkled in a smile.

I followed his line of sight to see Cora and my mother laughing together.

"She reminds me of my wife."

"Stubborn," murmured.

He chuckled. "Very much, and always gets her way."

"That's Cora."

"I want you to be careful with the Vargas Cartel deal. I know you put eyes in Mexico, but people can come up missing."

I gave him a stern look. "Savio made it clear to them that we have complete access to all the books and routes."

My father frowned. "So long as you know, being a lawyer is not only your job."

"I know, Pops."

"This lifestyle comes with a lot of responsibilities. I know I forced you boys to lead our legacy and make sacrifices."

"Cora's not angry with me anymore."

He grabbed his glass of scotch. "Do you regret it?"

I stood. "Sometimes, but it's in the past. We learn and grow."

"Family is the blood and strength you'll need one day when you become the Underboss."

I stilled at his words. "Is there something I need to know?"

"Savio came to talk to me about stepping down."

"He never mentioned it to me."

"Mckayla might be pregnant again."

"Sante would move into position as Don. Renato didn't want the Underboss role?"

My father waved off my comment. "Renato's too crazy."

I scanned the backyard. As if to prove my father's point, Renato had Bosco in a headlock.

"He's unpredictable. We need someone who keeps their emotions under control."

I inhaled a deep breath. "I'm not sure."

"You've been trained by the best. Sante will only want you to stand beside him."

My mind was a jumble of thoughts and emotions at this news. "Does Vincenzo know?"

"No. Nothing has been decided, but I want you to consider it and talk with Cora. Where are you going on this vacation?"

"How did you know about that?"

"I know everything, son."

I shook my head and returned to the party with a lot to think about.

* * *

I lifted my shades and smiled at Cora as she swam in the ocean. She grinned and motioned for me to join her. This was our first trip as a couple that she'd willingly joined me on without a fight.

A week after the party at my parent's house, we hopped on the plane to Bora Bora. We'd been here for two days. On the first day, we didn't get out of bed, and on the second, we went swimming and explored the area. I had a private chef and housekeeper on duty to handle our needs, and even Freddie was housed in the private cabana in the back. But we'd mostly been by ourselves.

Cora decided to cook breakfast this morning, and then we went to the ocean. Seeing her in her thong bikini was driving me crazy. I'd spent the day imagining peeling it from her body. I planned to lock her up in the bedroom tonight and have dinner delivered to our room.

"Are you going to get in the water?" she called.

"I like the view from here." My heated gaze captured hers.

"You like me naked, is all." She swiped the water from her eyes.

"I do," I murmured huskily.

She slid her tongue along her bottom lip. "Please, come get in the water."

"Those baby doll eyes get me every time."

"I know." She held her hand out for me.

I dove into the ocean and swam toward her. "Water feels good."

"It does. Where is your swimsuit?" I ran a hand along her naked back.

Cora lifted an eyebrow. "I tossed it a while ago. You weren't paying attention."

"Damn, you really want to get fucked out here." I chuckled., reaching for her hand.

She stretched her legs around my waist. "I do."

I grabbed her butt. "Vacation sex in the water."

Cora giggled. "Might as well explore more areas we can add to our list."

"Naughty girl." I pinched her ass cheek.

"This is just for you, EJ." She looped her arms around my neck.

"Fuck. I can't wait to get you back in the bedroom."

"Bedroom, ocean, tree. Anywhere with you is magical."

I nuzzled her neck. "We should live here forever."

She tilted her face to look at me. "You'd miss your family. I can hear Adelina now, crying about never seeing her grandbabies."

"They can visit."

Cora laughed. "You tell her that because I'm not."

My thumb caressed her bottom lip. "There's something I need to tell you."

"What's the matter?"

"My father asked me about moving up in the family business."

She didn't look surprised.

"Why do I feel like you knew about him asking me."

"Because Rena told me."

"How do you feel about me moving up as an Underboss?"

"The cartel broke us up, but we're older and wiser now. I understand the layers and how to navigate my role."

"I won't take it if you're against it. You're more important."

"I know, and I appreciate you considering my opinions, but I'm fully on board with being a Calabresi."

"Really, Cora?"

"Yes. I love you and know it comes with sacrifices. I won't let the past hold me back from loving you."

"You'll be loving an Underboss of the Calabresi Cartel."

"The wife of an Underboss sounds good to me."

My face split into a huge smile at hearing those words biggest smile and my heart overflowed with love. The little girl who stepped into my home with her mom that day and ignored me when I said hello was the best thing that had ever happened to me.

Cora tugged my head to hers, and we kissed all the way out of the ocean, across the sand, and into the bedroom. I professed my love over and over as she came endlessly on my tongue.

"Welcome to the family, my love."

Epilogue: Elio Jr
Christmas Eve one year later

My nieces and nephews ran around my house while the adults talked and laughed. Everybody joked about the last holiday events when I'd tried to kill Cora's date. But now we were celebrating Christmas in our own home as a housewarming party.

Cora did most of the decorating with her mom, who'd finally retired from working for our family. My father protested the amount of time the women spent at my house because he'd missed having his wife around.

I sipped on the cognac Renato had bought as a Christmas gift while the kids drank hot chocolate with the wives. Cora had gone shopping to ensure all the kids had gifts.

"You've got it bad, bro. Can't take your eyes off her," Renato joked as he joined me with Vincenzo and Sante. Savio was still the Don for the time being. Mckayla wasn't pregnant and didn't want him to step down, even though they were still trying for another baby. Renato and Sante always teased our parents, saying they enjoyed being grandparents even more than parents.

"Any updates?" I asked Sante.

"No issues. Payments are still rolling in like clockwork," Sante replied.

Renato was happy he no longer had to fly to Mexico to handle any problems. Months ago, we'd received word that one of our trucks full of product was stolen, and there was no word on who was behind it. I'd made inquiries and started sending escorts for the drop-offs, so we had people on border patrol on our team.

"He looks brand new." Renato motioned at Vincenzo.

I nodded. "He's been going out more than usual lately and bringing all types of girls around."

"I'll talk with him."

"No, you'll just start a fight," Sante muttered.

"He's my brother."

"I'm closer in age. I can talk to him," I offered.

"EJ! Are you ready for dinner?" Cora called.

"Sure. Maybe we can do gifts beforehand."

Cora put her glass on the table. "We can do that. The kids are ready to open gifts."

I grasped her hand, and we moved in front of the fireplace in the living room.

Cora cleared her throat to get everyone's attention. "Thank you all for coming here to spend the holiday together in our new home."

"It was her idea," I interjected, and she elbowed me in the side.

A knock at the door interrupted us.

"Who could that be?" Cora asked.

"Not sure. Let me go answer." Our new home wasn't far from my parent's property, and my security detail knew to keep me updated on any potential trouble. I opened the door to see Freddie holding a package.

"This was dropped at the gate," he said.

I took it and returned to the living room, turning the yellow envelope with no outgoing address.

"Open it," Cora said with a smile.

I unsealed and removed the pictures inside. "What am I looking at?" I asked, confused.

"The future child of Cora and EJ Calabresi," said softly.

My mouth dropped in surprise. "Wait...You're pregnant?"

She nodded. "Yes. About eight weeks."

"Why didn't you tell me?"

"I wanted to be sure. I checked with my doctor, and she confirmed."

"I'm going to be a father." I looked around the room at the smiling faces of my family.

The pictures were passed around, and everyone hugged and congratulated us.

"More grandbabies." Mom clapped her hands in delight.

I pulled Cora into my arms, whispering how much I loved her. "Seriously? We're having a baby?"

Cora glowed with happiness. "Yes, and I can't wait to see how you cope if it's a girl."

I grinned. "Might as well get the gun now."

* * *

I hope you enjoyed EJ and Cora's story. Check out the sneak peek of Vincenzo and Nyla coming soon.

Sneak Peek: Vincenzo

She did the unthinkable and now she has to pay.

She thought I wouldn't find her, but my reach runs far.

As the youngest son of Elio and Adelina Calabresi I make it my business to know everything about the people that come in contact with my family.

For many years my brothers tried to keep me out of the mafia business, but getting what's owed to me is my primary goal and I'm here to collect.

A debt owed, hate to love, forbidden, forced marriage, Dark Mafia romance, Book 5 in an interconnecting stand-alone series, and guaranteed to have an HEA.

Upcoming Releases

**Vincenzo
Giosuè
Armani
Bosco**

About the Author

L.K. Ryan is an author of Romantic Suspense, Dark Romance, and Contemporary Novels. Join my newsletter and sign up for the latest news and updates on my books and releases:

Calabresi Mafia Series

Savio: Book 1
https://books2read.com/u/mlEAW7
Sante: Book 2
https://books2read.com/u/mdd10W
Renato: Book 3
https://books2read.com/u/4AjAQd
Elio Jr: Book 4
https://books2read.com/u/4j5yjD
Vincenzo: Book 5

Thank you so much for reading. If you enjoyed the crazy ride and decide to leave a review, we'd appreciate the support.

9 781955 233422